GIRLS WILL BE GIRLS

ABOUT THE AUTHOR

Donald Wood was born into a mining family in Barnsley in 1937. Educated at Burton Road Junior School and Barnsley Holgate Grammar School, he then studied for a degree in Pharmacy at Cardiff University. In order to become a Member of the Pharmaceutical Society he completed post-graduate training in Hospital Pharmacy in Wakefield. Earlier, his first employment had been with Barnsley Borough Council as a sewerman's mate; so his working life started near the bottom, not at the bottom.

During the next few years he gained experience in Community Pharmacy, starting in Redcar, North Yorkshire, working as a shop manager for small companies and also as a locum pharmacist and medical representative. Leaving pharmacy for a period, he had a spell as a Maths and Science teacher in secondary education. In 1976 he opened his own chemist's shop near Barnsley, and is still employed running this business.

He is well known in sporting circles, having played soccer, cricket and badminton in the local leagues. Whilst at Barnsley Grammar he was School Cricket Captain, and also in 1953 captained the Barnsley Boys' cricket team, being capped for Yorkshire Boys in the same season.

He still plays badminton, made a come-back to cricket at the age of fifty, and is now helping out with the Barnsley third team.

Donald's other interests include reading, tennis, walking and the theatre.

He is a married man with two sons and a daughter.

GIRLS
will be
GIRLS

. . . and boys will be boys

by

Donald Wood

Illustrated by Frank McDiarmid

BRIDGE
PUBLICATIONS

PENISTONE · ENGLAND

Bridge Publications
2 Bridge Street, Penistone
Sheffield S30 6AJ

Illustrations copyright © Frank McDiarmid 1993

First Published 1993

ISBN 0-947934-30-8
ISBN 0-947934-29-4 Pbk

Photoset by Bridge Publications
Printed and bound in Great Britain by
Whitstable Litho Printers Ltd., Whitstable, Kent

for
Jane and Herbert
with love and thanks

PART ONE
SOUTH YORKSHIRE – 1965

1

A FEELING OF FRUSTRATION had been creeping into life for a good while. Activity had started to take on a mechanical, ritualistic, flavour – as though one did things in a certain way and, really, what other way could there possibly be? Most relationships were pretty static unless prodded violently by excesses of alcohol or tiredness. Even these weren't quite as effective as they used to be.

Such feelings had been working away inside Ken with a quiet persistence for the past two or three years, and always he'd been putting them off and deciding to give them more attention tomorrow. Tomorrow seemed much nearer as he sat at the bar of the local pub and asked the barmaid for another glass of bitter. It was Friday night, and he was glad that it was, because the week hadn't been a particularly smooth one. Not much had gone right at work, and he was looking forward to a weekend of sport and beer as welcome relief to re-charge the batteries. The barmaid refilled the glass and placed it on a soggy beer-mat in front of him. As she did so she smiled and remarked that things were quiet just at the moment, but she expected that when the match ended things would look up. He nodded his agreement and handed her a two shilling piece.

'Would you care for something?' he asked.

'That's very kind – I'll have a gin and tonic if I may.'

'Sure,' he said, hurriedly feeling in his pocket for more money. Before, she had been quite happy with a tomato juice, and as he searched his pocket he told himself to limit his benevolence with this particular barmaid to one gin and tonic. 'Getting mean in my old age,' he thought to himself, mildly amused at himself for having reacted like this. By the time he'd found the deficit she had poured the gin and added half the tonic water, and was about to take the first sip.

'All the best, love,' she said.

'Cheers,' he replied, raising his glass and simultaneously placing a ten-shilling note on the bar. Pocketing the change he said, 'You'll always have fine healthy kidneys.'

She looked mystified and not at all interested – the response he'd hoped to evoke.

To explain himself he continued, 'You see, I believe gin is flavoured with juniper, and medicinal preparations of juniper have been used down the ages to alleviate backache and kidney complaints.'

The mystified look changed into one of blank wonder, followed by, 'Oh!' This seemed to be a polite substitute for, 'What sort of crank is this? Fancy talking about my kidneys! What next?'

At this moment two chaps entered and came up to the bar. They were dressed in overalls, their faces unwashed, and they had obviously just finished work.

The barmaid greeted them, 'Late tonight boys, aren't we?'

The shorter of the two pushed his cap back off his forehead and replied, 'It's always a busy day Friday luv. Two of the best.'

Before he'd finished speaking she'd placed one pint in front of them and half filled another.

'She don't need no telling, this lass,' said the other chap, who had rested both his elbows on the bar and was gazing intently at her as she waited for the froth to settle a little before giving the pump another short pull to complete the operation.

'There we are, Fred, just what the doctor ordered, eh?'

2

"Tis that.' 'Ave been ready for this since eight this morning.'

They proceeded to drink half way down the glasses without a pause.

'It's grand, is that.'

'Best pint for miles around here,' they said, looking around the bar for confirmation of these views.

Spotting an acquaintance at the far end of the bar, they picked up their pots and joined him. The barmaid took her glass and went to talk to them.

Ken felt a certain amount of relief at this, as he had no desire to continue the conversation already started. He much preferred to pass the time of day and leave it at that. He was now able to listen and observe – a situation that afforded plenty of satisfaction. He sipped at his beer, his third in the last half hour, and strained to try and overhear the joke that one of the workmen was soon relating. He recognized it as one he'd heard before, and on its completion was surprised that it was received with such a show of hilarity. The three men laughed out loud and the barmaid pretended to be shocked.

By now the beer had started to take effect, and he was feeling a little light-headed. He was puzzled at this as it normally took three or four pints, not halves, to produce such a sensation. He put it down to the fact that he hadn't had a large or good evening meal. His mother, who was widowed, and with whom he lived, had been on holiday for a fortnight, and meals had turned out to be a bit of a problem. At first he'd managed quite well, going to all kinds of trouble to maintain the standards to which he was accustomed. But after a week things had started to deteriorate. It all seemed too much trouble. He got a good dinner in the canteen at the glassworks where he worked, so he made that do. Breakfast had become cornflakes and a cup of coffee as opposed to the cereals or porridge, bacon, sausages, eggs and goodness knows what else that

3

a devoted mother provided.

He thought about his mother. He realized that, on the whole, he had no cause for complaint. He was well fed (only grilled steak was good enough for lunch if he was playing soccer or cricket in the afternoon), he had a comfortable home, an immaculately ironed shirt available at all times, and all the creature comforts he could ask for. He supposed that these counter-balanced the limiting, claustrophobic, effect she tried to impose from time to time. He also supposed that it was probably only natural, since his father had died eighteen months ago. Before, everything was certain and ordered, and the purpose clear. But now the foundation had been eroded, and this must not be allowed to go any further.

For the first six months after his father's death he'd let things pass, just to keep the peace. But of late that had become increasingly more difficult. The odd outbursts of temper, on both sides, had started to manifest themselves. The holiday had arrived in the nick of time to prevent a big explosion. A cooling-off period was much needed. His thoughts were now engaged on how he was going to handle the coming weeks. He had to think long and hard about his parents to be able to do this. He had to try to understand and make sense of the past if he was to do what he wanted to do without too much upheaval. This was leading to a meandering nostalgic journey (alcohol, combined with relative solitude, rarely failed to do this), when he was suddenly jolted back to the present.

'Good game didn't you think? Have you been down?'

'Hello Ray, you old drunk. No. They're beyond redemption.'

'What was the score?'

'Three one, and a well deserved win. Ready for one?'

'Please.'

'Three pints love, please,' he shouted to the barmaid.

'Three, why three?' Ken asked.

'Tony's with me. Had to make a quick dash to the back; he supped too many at half-time.'

'Doesn't he know we've got a match tomorrow?'

'He'll be OK. He's a fit lad is Tony.'

It was early September, and the local soccer leagues were starting their fixtures. The cricket season was drawing to its all-too-soon close, and this posed problems. Good soccer players tended to be good cricketers, so priorities at this time of year were often difficult to agree. Some wanted to play cricket, some soccer. Team selection was no fun.

They were joined by Tony and three other chaps who had been to the match. In a second Ken saw the next two hours. About an hour would be spent analysing why and how the score had ended up as it did, why the manager had made a blunder in picking such and such a player, and who ought to play in the next game. Then there would be a general discussion about the sporting events of the week, and finally jokes and women would come into their own. Although so predictable, everyone – or so it appeared by the interest shown and the eagerness to take part – enjoyed these weekly get-togethers. The beer flowed freely, and so everything was viewed through a pleasant alcoholic haze. The time was passing much as usual, and the team to play the following week had been finalized. The bar had filled with men from the match and some regular Friday night couples. The barmaids were pulling pints as fast as was possible, aided by the publican – who had come in when the place became crowded. His main function was standing and chatting, and for light relief he occasionally condescended to pour a light ale or milk stout. Ken had painfully discovered that he was happy when holding forth on his pet subjects of fishing and himself, but didn't care to listen to – or show interest in – anyone else's opinions. He had a well-established trade and so was able to indulge himself in this way. He never watched soccer, but criticized the local side with relish. His sense of his own importance seemed to be increased when doing this. Things weren't going too well for him tonight, because Ray happened to think that the 'Reds' had made a good start to the season and intended that others should feel the same way.

'Your opinion's worthless, anyway. You haven't watched 'em for years,' said Ray.

Knowing Ray, interesting developments looked like taking place. On one occasion, during a closely fought cup-tie, he had offered to urinate in an opposition fan's hat, so that perhaps then he'd be less inclined to talk through it. The offer wasn't accepted, the reply being a kick on the shins. Ray replied with an uppercut, and the police stepped in five minutes later. Some sort of victory gained in spite of losing the tie. So, with little provocation, Ray tended to explode from time to time. This situation had all the appearance of such an outburst being possible.

Four pints swallowed in quick time, a strongly held belief, and the weekend just starting. It looked inevitable. In company such as this it would probably take the form of a juicy cursing exchange. Knowing winks and nods passed between the company.

'They're always as bad, so why waste time and money going to see them?' the publican replied.

'How would you know that, pray, if you admit you never go? You're just showing your ignorance.'

'I was watching 'em before you were born, so you can't tell me owt I don't already know.'

'Well, if that's supposed to indicate that a feeling of creeping senility alone can settle an argument, you're even simpler than I suspected.' Ray was obviously pleased that he'd thought of saying this, and looked around for approval.

Not easily put off, the publican continued, scornfully, 'Yer long fancy words don't impress me,' staring Ray

Your opinion's worthless, anyway.

straight in the eye.

'I can translate if you wish,' Ray replied, staring him out.

'Ugh! Translate? It's a transfer you want to talk about. Start with the chairman and the directors, and you'll be getting somewhere.'

'Have you ever had a good word to say about anything?'

'Look, sonny, are you trying to be funny?' he said, moving forward and pushing his head nearer to Ray's in a menacing manner.

'Look, grandad, I'm not your sonny. You can call me Mister, Sir, or something equally respectful, but please – not sonny. It'll give people the wrong idea.'

'Any more cheek from you . . . ' he started, when he was interrupted by a waiter with a request for six pints, a babycham, and a vodka and lime.

He looked irritated at not being able to finish his threat, and glanced about him to see if anyone else was free to serve. They were all busy, and he skulked away to draw the beer, muttering inaudibly as he did so.

'Pack it in Ray,' Tony advised. 'You know you'll get no sense out of him.'

'It's interesting though. Reminds me that I've still got blood in my veins.'

'Shows that your blood alcohol level is sky high you mean,' said Tony.

'Hark at this. An engineer with a knowledge of blood alcohol levels,' said Ken.

'Can't you tell we've got a sexy red-headed Minister of Transport. At long last the message is getting through. Old Wilson must have realized that sex can sell road safety as well as cigarettes and cars,' said Tony, laughing.

'Tell them why, then,' said Ken.

Ray coloured a little and took a long drink of his beer. Everyone looked at him expectantly. He put his glass down and looked up at them.

'What do you mean?' he asked, innocently, looking at Ken.

'I've got a good memory, mate. Come on, stop hedging,' replied Ken.

'It's nothing really. I know what Ken's referring to, but it isn't the reason I've been out with one or two redheads in my time.'

He paused, and took another drink.

'Well?' said Tony.

'It's nowt, believe me.'

'Let's have it.'

'Well, you know that bike shop I used to work in on Saturday afternoons when I was still at school? The manager was quite a lad and talked incessantly about sex. One day he said that he'd only been out with one redhead in his life, and that she was as ugly as hell. The reason he took her out was to satisfy his curiosity. He'd always wondered whether the hair was red in – what shall we say – other less accessible parts.'

'And was it?' asked Tony.

'That's just it. The manager wouldn't tell him, so he's been carrying out one or two investigations of his own,' said Ken.

They all laughed.

'Get lost,' said Ray, not amused.

'I expect you'll get a doctorate for it,' said Tony. 'I can see it now on the front page of the South Yorkshire Observer: 'Raymond Goodall has been awarded a degree for his studies into the morphology, habitat and pigmentation of the concealed appendages of the red-headed female of the species homo sapiens.'

'Very funny,' replied Ray, still finding it difficult to see the funny side of it. Ray was good at giving it out, but didn't like being on the receiving end.

The publican had by this time placed the drinks on a tray and, as he handed it to the waiter, said something and

9

smirked in Ray's direction.

The waiter nodded his agreement.

Ray noticed that he was being discussed, and saluted them.

The publican said something else, his expression suggesting that Ray's gesture served as a perfect endorsement for all that he'd said previously.

At this, Ray picked up his glass and toasted them.

'Cheers!' he shouted. And then, after he'd taken a drink, grimaced to show his disapproval of the brew. The publican tossed his head into the air with disdain and walked away to talk to a group of men who were sitting at a table in the middle of the room, playing cards.

The conversation now returned to its original groove. Someone had started relating the latest joke about the Indians and Pakistanis in the district. Ken had never been able to understand why these jokes, which as jokes were usually very feeble, always produced an exaggerated response from the listeners. Perhaps, he thought, it was some sort of inferiority complex which could only be salved by deflating as often as possible the cause of the irritation. Whereas some of the young toughs of the town had no inhibitions about a punch-up as a release to their pent-up feelings, a thump in the ribs with a mocking joke was all the majority were allowed. He remembered having read somewhere that it all boiled down to sexual jealousy, that the white man thought that the black man was much the better lover and never suffered the agonies of impotence. The article had proceeded to show that this wasn't the case, and proffered the theory that sexual activity was more likely to be proportional to a man's I.Q. than to the colour of his skin. The brainier you are the sexier you are. He visualized a stage being reached when a well-meaning sociologist would produce a graph which would indicate with whom it was appropriate to make love. And if this didn't produce gratification, well there was always plenty

10

of pleasure to be had constructing graphs.

The joke had reached its climax and, in reply to the question, 'Well, what is brown, has two balls and rings a bell?' the teller supplied the answer – 'A Pakistani bus conductor.'

Beer sprayed everywhere as laughter acted as a pump to the mouthful taken in before the joke's completion. This reminded someone of a similar one, and so concentration was given solely to him.

By this time, Ken wasn't enjoying the proceedings. He felt a bit tipsy and wasn't looking forward to drinking another two pints of beer – which had to be accepted for sociability's sake. Looking around the bar, the only thing he seemed to be able to see were masses of people swallowing dark brown liquid, the liquid going on its journey through the body, finally being excreted, then evaporating, condensing and the whole cycle starting again. It had all the appearances of a vicious circle. And yet in their lives these people, like the fluid, appeared resigned to the fact that this was all in the way of things. To stick to the circumference was to accept the known and the comfortable.

Just how you could leave the safe path of the circumference was something Ken hadn't seriously thought about, but he realized that the time was fast approaching when he would have to.

With a conscious effort he forced his attention back to the joke, glancing from face to face at the anticipatory expressions.

As it ended, a middle-aged gentleman tapped Ray on the shoulder.

'I suppose you'll be happy with tonight's result, Mr Goodall?' he said.

'Hello, Mr Sedgwick,' replied Ray, looking surprised. 'Yes, a good game and a very satisfactory result. They certainly needed the points. Can I get you something?'

'Thanks. I'll have a gill, if I may.'

Ray ordered it, and turning back said, 'I don't think you've met my friends, Mr Sedgwick, have you?'

'No, I don't think I have.'

'Lads, I'd like you to meet my headmaster, the man who keeps my nose to the grindstone,' and he quickly went round the group, mentioning their names.

There were too many of them to shake hands and, when Ray had finished, Mr Sedgewick said, 'Pleased to meet you all. One or two of you look familiar. I wouldn't be surprised if I didn't teach your parents during the earlier stages of my career. I taught at Highfields Junior for five years.'

'I didn't know you frequented this pub, sir,' said Ray, who was immediately at ease with him.

'Well, I don't as a rule. My wife has a sister who lives just along the road from here, and when the talk got onto women's underwear I thought it an opportune moment to skip out for a breath of fresh air. The walk gave me a thirst, so I thought I'd just pop in for a quick one. I must say that I'm rather pleased I've bumped into you, as I'm not one who enjoys going into pubs on my own. It's not that I crave company, but I get the feeling that when you are on your own it looks as though you are there just for the booze. I enjoy a drink, but a change of scene and a chat are the main reasons for my visiting a pub.'

This was greeted with one or two mutterings of 'Yes, I agree,' although if pressed the ones saying this would have had to put the beer first and the chat and scene change a poor second.

A readjustment had now to be made. They were all well-oiled, and the talk flowing wherever it wished; but with the introduction of a sober figure more care had to be taken. It wasn't easy.

'Talking about people around here, have you spent most of your career in this district?' asked Ray.

12

'I have, actually. I'm born and bred in these parts; all my working life has been spent in Barnfield and district. I've often thought that I should have moved about more, but mainly I've been quite content. And you know promotion's a bit easier if you happen to be a local lad come good,' he said, smiling.

'How long have you been a headmaster?'

'Oh! Let me see. It must be getting on for ten years now. That's it. I started at Highfields Junior, then ten years in secondary schools at Hope Street and Minehead Central, and I got the head's job at Bradstone in 1954. I'd better stop. I'm giving my age away.'

'I'll tell you this,' said Ray, 'I'm on the worst deal as a teacher because all these plutocrats can gad about in cars while I have to rely on good old Mr Exley's public transport. Being a chemist, engineer or bank clerk certainly seems a paying game,' Ray continued.

'My heart bleeds for you,' said Tony. 'The fact is that we live way above our means, and if the Chancellor decides to have a credit squeeze all our affluence goes for a Burton.'

'Listen, mate, I live above my means–and I can hardly afford a bike,' said Ray.

'You know, the salary gets better in time, and you have a job which gives a lot of satisfaction,' said Mr Sedgwick.

'I agree, and admit that I'm happy doing what I'm doing and have never regretted having chosen teaching as a career, but it annoys me that society doesn't value, in hard cash, what I'm doing as highly as it does many things that strike me as useless or at least not as important.'

'Pass him his soapbox,' someone said.

'What are you comparing it with?' asked Mr Sedgwick.

'Well, a pal I went to school with travels the country persuading shopkeepers to buy a certain brand of biscuit. For this he earns approximately twice the salary I get and has a car thrown in as well.'

13

'Ray for Prime Minister,' a voice from the back said.

'I'd have more idea than most of that lot in Parliament.'

'At least you're doing a job you like. Most people spend their lives in a boring sort of occupation. To do something you believe in with a certain amount of passion – surely this is important in life . . . ' Ken said.

'Pass Ken the pulpit,' was the rejoinder from the back.

'What do you do Ken?' asked Mr Sedgwick.

'I'm a chemist at the glassworks, which of course is a good job. An uncle of mine came to see us not long ago and he asked me what I did. I told him, and you could tell by the expression on his face just what he thought about it. He conjured up a picture of middle-class respectability; nine to five, well-dressed, staff entrance and on speaking terms with the Works Manager. These things he obviously had a high regard for. He didn't ask if I enjoyed it or found it stimulating. Work, it appears, isn't intended to do any of these things.'

'I would expect that a lot of what you do is repetitive,' said Mr Sedgwick.

'That is so. What you have to do once the basic work has been mastered is to look for interesting things to focus upon. In a way that's the good thing about it. There is enough time available to be able to do this.'

'You'll have a degree, so you're not tied. Teaching's always looking out for science graduates, you know,' his face breaking into a broad grin.

'Yes, I have a degree, but I only graduated three years ago. And as the firm gave me a fair bit of help in one way and another I feel obliged to stay with them a while. I don't have to, of course. There's no compulsion of any kind.'

'You've got a point, but I wouldn't let it be too restrictive. Should you be inclined towards teaching, come and see me if you wish. I would be pleased to give you any advice that I can.'

14

'It had crossed my mind, and Ray and I have discussed it from time to time ... but it's the money,' Ken replied, smiling sheepishly at his final comment.

'It has its compensations, like I said before,' Mr Sedgwick answered, glancing at his watch and then emptying his glass. 'Well, I must be on my way. Mustn't be late for supper. I'm pleased to have met you all. Good night.'

And with that he made his way from the bar. Before leaving he approached the barmaid and ordered a round of drinks.

'Do you want them now?' the barmaid shouted down the bar.

'Might as well luv, we'll sup up,' replied Tony.

'Seems a pleasant chap, Ray,' said Ken.

'Yes, I like him a lot. He's given me stacks of help over the last few months. When I first started there I was unsure of myself and tried much too hard. As a result my discipline wasn't all that it should have been and it didn't take him long to notice. He started coming into my lessons on some pretext or other, and the next thing I knew we were both taking the lesson – or rather he was taking the lesson and I was picking up the tricks of the trade from him. The kids didn't really realize what was happening, and just thought it novel and a pleasant diversion. I admired him for doing it that way. From what you hear, not all headmasters are so considerate. Things are much better now, but he still pops in from time to time.'

'What's his subject?' asked Tony.

'Maths, but it appears he's at home with most things. He speaks French fluently, and often lets the French woman have a free period. He hasn't a degree, but that's only because grants were hard to come by in his day. It's rumoured that he was a bit of a lad for the girls in his younger days – that is until his wife heard about it. The small blot about him is his politics – red from top to bottom. Got to be, to get a head's job in this town, you

15

know.'

'That makes him a perfectly rounded fellow,' said Ken, good humouredly.

Tony then jumped in. 'Let's leave it at that, shall we lads? Ten o'clock on a Friday night with beer still left in the barrel is not time to be talking politics. Same again all round Mary, love, please,' he shouted, and then drained his pot, which was half full, at one gulp.

'Mary ... love ... please?' said Ray, looking at him with raised eyebrows. 'Since when has it been Mary, love, please? Look at that–she's serving us straight away and there are at least four chaps up yonder who've been waiting gagging for ten minutes.'

'Oh, drop it,' said Tony, mildly irritated.

'She looks willing,' said Ray. 'And let's face it, you're willing anytime Tony mate, so what are you waiting for?'

Tony was embarrassed and looked away with no intention of replying, and obviously hoping that would be the end of it. As she placed the tray in front of them, Ray grabbed her hand before she could release her grip.

'This, my dear, in case you don't know, is Anthony, better known to his friends as Tony, and you may call him love if you wish.'

'Charmed, I'm sure. Why don't you look after yourself and let other people do the same?'

Not easily deterred, Ray replied.

'The facts of life, Mary love, are such that it isn't everyone that can manage these things on their own, and extroverts such as yours truly are required to supply the grease from time to time so that the wheels don't clog up altogether. I feel that I'm performing a humble service for my fellow men.'

'Take no notice, Mary. He often gets carried away with the sound of his own voice, and if he could only see straight he's the one in need of the outside help,' said Tony.

16

'It's alright Tony, it doesn't bother me, see you later.'

And with that she moved away to continue serving.

'See you later,' said Ray. 'Is there really anything between you two then?'

'As a matter of fact I have taken her home once or twice, but there's nothing serious about it. She happens to be more sensible than you suspect. So for Christ's sake let's leave it at that.'

'What bothers me is that she's a married woman, separated from her husband, and this could implicate you in all kinds of things. I don't think too badly of her, she's attractive, in the right places and, as barmaids go, well above average intelligence. The few times I've been in here alone I've found her good company,' said Ray.

'I know she's married. She told me all about it herself, so there's no deceit on her part. And I'm not likely to be so foolish as to get so involved that I'd get raked into any divorce proceedings. Anyway, she reckons she should have her divorce through in about six months time.'

'What are the grounds?' asked Ken.

'Oh, he went off with one of the girls who worked in the shoeshop he managed. Left the town completely. First stop London, and now God knows where. Apparently things hadn't worked out too well from the start, and it wasn't long before he started leaving the straight and narrow. You'll probably know him. He managed the shop at the bottom of King Street.'

'Yes, I think I know the chap,' said Ray. 'Tall, fair-haired, with thick-rimmed glasses. Doesn't look particularly attractive to women.'

'That's the one. It's funny you should say that, because I remarked about the same thing to Mary. His charm creeps over them slowly.'

'Dirty devil,' flashed Ray, drawing laughter all round.

'He's got quite a way with the ladies, apparently. Picks 'em up without any trouble.'

17

'Talking about picking things up,' said Ray, 'what about these two who've just appeared?'

All heads, without discretion, turned in the direction of the door.

'Look nice, but a bit young and not too bright I would say,' added Tony.

'Since when have you been so choosy?' asked Ray. 'Must be Mary that's raised his standards. Move over then, make a bit of room for the fair sex,' he added as the girls moved towards the bar.

'Good evening girls,' said Ray as the girls reached the only space available.

The first of the girls, who was a bottle blonde and a replica of forty other girls to be seen any Saturday morning walking around the town, replied.

'I don't suppose it's us that you're talking to, is it?'

'Could be just that,' said Ray.

'Forget it in that case!' replied the blonde.

'Touchy aren't we dear?' said Ray.

'Nothing of the sort, it's just that I'm not used to being accosted by drunks,' came the reply.

'Takes more than four pints to get me drunk, love.'

'Well, if that's your half-drunk state I'm not too fond of that either,' she replied, turning and asking the barman for two milk stouts.

He quickly handed them the drinks, and after declining Ray's offer to pay they moved to the other end of the room without disguising their pleasure at being able to get away from the company at the bar.

'You ought to be more aware of your position, you know,' said Tony. 'Chatting up anything that came along was alright as an undergraduate, but a staid respected member of the teaching profession, as you are now, should set an example and keep his baser instincts under control. Take me, for instance. I'm an engineer, and my public image never slips.'

All heads turned in the direction of the door.

'Does it allow you to go about with barmaids?' asked Ray, rather sarcastically.

'Of course it does!' An engineer is, according to the adverts, a tough, virile, super-masculine type who hits the world with a bang. More or less anything goes, including the odd indiscretion with a barmaid. That was the hardest part of the training, developing the persona.'

'How do you see us? As a cross between a priest and a politician full of anaemia and righteousness?' asked Ray.

'Pretty near the mark. You are expected to give a lead in everything you do. Take how you speak – there must be none of this lapsing into broad Yorkshire. You must be sober in dress – beards are out – and even the female company you keep must conform to this pattern. In their case moustaches are out, or else. Be seen with a floosy from the wrong end of town and you become something of an oddball who hasn't absorbed the rules of the game. You've got my sympathy!'

'It's not so bad, although it does tend to get a bit that way. As for chatting up the women – it's an addiction that's hard to give up.'

'Aren't there any eligible frustrated domestic science or P.T. mistresses pining for your attention?' asked Ken.

'Big deal. There is one young lady I rather like the look of, but I arrived on the scene about two years too late. The purveyor of artistic culture picked her up as soon as she arrived. I keep telling her she's much too good for him, but she only smiles and doesn't take any notice. She thinks I'm just teasing, and has no idea of the consuming passion that I have for her,' he finished, dejectedly resting his head on his hand, supporting his elbow on a dry part of the bar.

'You look consumed, standing there, thirteen and a half stone of unadulterated fat,' said Tony.

'Is she going to marry the bloke?' asked Ken.

'They're not engaged, but I fear it won't be long. It'll be

an awful waste. He's an egocentric who has a thing about art. He has the idea that he's a cut above the rest of us because the Royal Academy didn't accept him. I'd only been there a week before I knew that he'd studied at the Chelsea School of Art, obtained his Dip. Ed. at Sheffield, and then applied to the Royal Academy. The fact that he'd been interviewed by the keepers of the Queen's Art obviously satisfied his pride and allowed him to be elevated above the mob.'

'You're getting greener every second,' said Tony.

'Another drink?' asked Ken. 'It's almost half past ten.'

Most of the pots were still quite full, and they all agreed that enough was enough. Another joke was told to round off the evening, and the pub started to slowly empty.

'Come on, let's go. Mustn't miss the wrestling on the old box,' said Tony, moving towards the door.

'What about tomorrow? Are we at home?' asked Ken.

'Away at Scarsthorpe. Be there for half past two at the latest. And by the way, there are some changes from last week. Mainly positional, but not too popular I bet. We've put you at full-back, Peter at wing-half, and young Johnny at centre-forward,' replied Ray.

'Sounds OK to me, considering the last two performances. I can't see how anyone can complain, though putting Johnny in the thick of things in a cup match could turn out tricky. Scarsthorpe are cloggers to a man if they get behind.'

'This selection business gets worse every week. It took us all night and five pints to pick tomorrow's team.'

'What are your chances?' asked someone, who didn't play himself but followed the team with a sadistic kind of pleasure. 'Is it going to be four or six nil this week?'

'Cheeky sod,' said Ray. 'We've an even chance if we can regain our earlier form, if the ground isn't too heavy and if everybody turns up.'

'Considering the ifs, it sounds like twenty to one

21

against.'

'You're forgetting one thing mate. The Scarsthorpe players will sup four or five pints before going on the field. The thing to do against these sides is to pile it on in the first half, and hope that by the time they come round in the second half they're too far behind to catch up. In a league match last year we were winning three nowt at half-time and managed to lose six four. This we put down to the sobering up as the game went on and to an ineffectual referee who let the crowd intimidate him to such an extent that the game became almost a free-for-all. He put his whistle in his pocket and left it there.'

Once outside the pub, a cool breeze soon had them making for home.

'See you tomorrow Ken,' said Ray. 'Don't be late again. I get butterflies as it is, and when you turn up two minutes before the kick-off I'm like a nervous wreck.'

'I'll try not to be, as it's a cup game. Anyway, I didn't know you got nervous before a game?'

'What! I have a crap four times, without fail, every Saturday morning.'

'So do I, but that's the Friday night beer.'

'Don't tell me you're not a bit on edge before a game,' said Tony.

'I am, I must admit. That probably explains why I usually turn up late.'

'Why?, asked Tony. 'Can't you drag yourself out of the toilet?'

'Much as I enjoy a crap, that isn't the whole reason. I hate standing about waiting beforehand, and by being late I get ready, go out, and start playing. Once I've touched the ball the confidence oozes back into me.'

'The ooze hasn't been noticeable of late,' said Ray.

'It hasn't in any of us for that matter.'

'Ooze and booze don't mix, gentlemen,' said Tony.

'Hah, hah, hah,' said Ray.

'Be fair. I'm trying in spite of being drunk.'

'Why don't you come and watch us for once?' said Ken to Mike, the super-critic.

'I might just do that.'

'It's moral support we want, mate, not sexual support,' said Ray.

'Who's being funny now then?'

'Just stating a fact,' said Ray. 'if you played for us you'd need a left boot, a right boot, and an extra large middle boot.'

'Don't think they make a size thirteen,' added Ken.

'Just because I was fortunate enough to be in the front of the queue when they were handed out there's no need for this professional jealousy.'

'Jealous. I'm not jealous,' said Ray. 'If I was a woman and you produced that thing I'd go down on my knees and plead for mercy, and failing that I'd run for the nearest carving knife.'

'Like I said, professional jealousy. Nobody's complained so far.'

'That's because they haven't survived to tell the tale.'

'There's a joke about this,' said Ken. 'Two negroes standing on the bank of a river. One leans down and dips his hand into the water. "It's cold, man." The other takes out his old man and dips that in. "Deep, too," he says.'

'Go back to sleep,' said Ray.

'That's definitely my cue to go,' said Tony.

With that they departed.

2

THE FRESH AIR had cleared Ken's head a little, and he walked slowly down the road, swaying slightly from side to side. By this time the streets were almost deserted, except for the odd person returning from the fish and chip shop. This had a long queue of near-intoxicated men who, not content with making themselves almost sick with beer, thought they'd complete the process with a fish and a bobsworth of chips. It was a weekend ritual in this part of the town. How they managed to come up bright and perky and ready for another session by the following lunchtime, Ken had never been able to fathom. As he got nearer to the street in which he lived, he decided to sit on the wall that ran down the side of the main road. He thought that another ten minutes would help him to eliminate the sway altogether. He usually encountered someone who lived in their street when returning home at this hour, and as this would necessitate a short chat he wanted to be in the best possible condition under the circumstances. Few of the people in the street visited the local pubs. It was just about the most sedate street in the district. The gardens were well kept, the privet cut every Sunday morning, the odd car washed every Sunday afternoon and, to ease a slight guilt complex, *Songs of Praise* was a must after Sunday tea. They gossipped, but rarely maliciously. Furniture, wallpaper, sport, children, grandchildren, clothes, price rises, what the doctor said when they visited him, and such like, were the main topics. They wanted the best possible for their children.

It was slowly dawning on him that North Dene had been a good district in which to have been brought up. He looked around the town, and on reflection felt fortunate that fate (or rather the fact that the landlord of the houses had found their previous house clean and well-kept and the rent book not in arrears) had planted him in such an environment. It was a working-class district, but not cripplingly so. There had been pains to endure and overcome at the local grammar school, but they were certainly not insurmountable. In fact the thing to guard against, once the battles were won, was arrogance. And likewise at University there was a short period of adjustment and then a fairly smooth and enjoyable passage.

He eased himself off the wall, took a few deep breaths, straightened his tie, and set off down the road. His balance had improved, and with hard concentration he was able to proceed in a manner which wouldn't give rise to the slightest suspicion of his semi-drunkenness. On the other side of the road three young couples were sauntering along arm in arm in the opposite direction. For every four paces forward they took two or three back, so that progress was slow. They were talking loudly, and obviously enjoying every second of it. Friday night was the best night for dances in the town and, as the last buses were about ten o'clock, most of them had to walk home. Ken recognized one of the lads as an apprentice at the works. He had a cheerful personality, without a trace of shyness. He hadn't noticed Ken.

'Had a good night, then?' shouted Ken.

The lad turned and, instantly recognizing him, shouted back.

'What do you think?' putting both arms around his girlfriend and squeezing her hard. 'It's not over yet, either!' he said, kissing her full on the lips. They all laughed out loud.

'So long, then.'

'So long,' they all replied in unison.

As he reached the top of the street he turned right, almost walking into a gas-lamp post which was situated just around the corner.

'Perhaps I do look drunk, after all,' he muttered to himself.

With a further effort at control he set off down the street. Approaching him about fifty yards away he saw a man and woman who lived near the top of the street. He didn't know them well, but enough for them to stop and ask him how he was getting on, how his mother was keeping, etc. He wasn't looking forward to it one little bit. 'As I approach them I'll keep looking at the floor until we're only two or three yards apart. That way I can just say goodnight and keep on walking,' he argued to himself.

The plan was working well. The sway was conquered, the line of approach straight, the gaze uninterruptedly hard at a point on the pavement three inches in front of his shoes. When three yards separated them he thought, 'Perfect, couldn't have worked better.'

Then all was shattered!

'Your mother's had lovely weather for her holiday, Ken,' the woman said.

'Oh! Hello! Yes she has,' he replied, a little awkwardly.

By now they were face to face. He was determined not to say anything that might prolong the encounter, and added no more.

'Where has she been to, Scarborough was it?' asked the woman.

'No. Rhyl, as a matter of fact.'

'Oh Rhyl? We were there two years ago, weren't we Fred?'

'Yes,' said Fred.

'Lovely spot it is,' she continued. 'You get better weather on that coast. And it's so clean, and the people are so friendly. That's what I always think.'

'I suppose you're right, although to be honest I've never been myself. It was always Scarborough or Bridlington when I was a boy.'

'Coming back tomorrow, is she?'

26

He was determined not to prolong the encounter.

'Yes.'

'Well, it'll have done her good, a nice rest like that. I don't blame her for getting away when she can.'

'No.'

'Who has been looking after you then Ken?'

'Oh, I've managed for myself, after a sorts.'

'You look as though you've lost a bit of weight,' said Fred, laughing.

'Wouldn't be surprised at that,' replied Ken, patting his stomach.

'It must be nice for your mother to have you at home again. It must have been lonely for her after your dad died, and you at college an' all,' the woman added.

'She's got a lot of friends, though.'

'She has, that's true.'

'Do you intend settling around here, Ken?' asked Fred.

'Haven't made up my mind yet. It'll depend on several factors.' As he said this he turned slightly and shuffled a couple of paces down the street.

'Well, I must be off. Got to wash all this week's milk bottles and cups and saucers before the lady of the house gets back.'

'I bet you're not joking either,' she said, laughing.

'I'm not,' he replied, walking away.

'Good night!' they shouted.

'Good night!'

'Not so bad,' he thought. 'Probably reeked like a brewery, but otherwise OK.'

He now walked quickly, reached the gate, went down the alley to the back door, took out his key, and entered the small lobby at the bottom of the stairs. The front door was only used by the postman and the paper boy. Another door led into the room that acted as living room, dining room, kitchen, and where the washing was done. And this room only being four yards by three yards in dimensions. In one corner was a sink, and next to this a gas hob with two rings. Next, on the same wall, was his mother's pride and joy, a fire range – the coal fire with an oven attached. Down the chimney hung a rod, which could be adjusted so that the flames and heat of the fire could be directed to the oven when this was required. At other times the flames were allowed to go straight up, so that more heat entered the room. Also, two adjustable rings were situated so that a kettle or pans could be placed on them and the fire used to boil the kettle or cook the contents of the pans – usually vegetables or fish, when having boiled fish for dinner or supper. All this was necessary in the cause of economy. Ken's father had been a coal miner, and coal was cheaper for them than gas. In fact they always had a surplus of coal, so they were able to supply a neighbour who wasn't a miner with coal. In return Ken's father received work clothes and boots which were supplied to this man free at his place of work. Perhaps it was illegal, but just about everybody in the street had a similar arrangement operating. The oven and the fireplace were blackleaded and polished religiously every Friday morning and sometimes in between if necessary. The flues had to be similarly attended to on a weekly basis, to ensure the efficiency of the oven. If this wasn't done the home-made bread and bread-cakes were the first to suffer in quality, closely followed by the Yorkshire puddings. One easy chair, three ordinary chairs, a table and a sideboard, were the only pieces of furniture. A door on the wall opposite to the fire led into the pantry. Into the recess at the side of the fire had been built cupboards to hold the crockery. Another door led into the front room, which was only used occasionally – at weekends and on special occasions – if visitors arrived and more space was required. This room had a tiled fireplace, a three piece suite, a china cabinet, and a highly polished table. It was kept in lovely decorative order, his mother insisting on changing the wallpaper very regularly in spite of his father's protestations. Ken had used this room when doing his homework at week-ends.

The living room had family photographs and a plaster Alsatian dog on the sideboard, and a tea-caddy, pipe-rack and letter-rack on the mantlepiece. A cosy room. The most important item, though, was the Philips wireless, placed on a small table in one corner. Later a 12-inch television set was found a place on the sideboard. This had been obtained on rental just in time to see the 1953 'Matthews Cup Final'. Friends and neighbours had crowded in to see this event, and something happened that had everybody talking and laughing about it for years to come. The match was talked about for years, but so was this incident. At a particularly exciting point in the game, one of the men watching, who had a tendency to get very wrapped up and carried away with things, dived across the room to try and save a shot at goal by Blackpool's Stan Mortensen. Everybody laughed. The man was a little embarrassed, and apologized. Mortensen's shot just went wide. A day to remember, a match to remember.

Another day to remember, a little later that year, was the Queen's Coronation. On that occasion all the women crowded around the television set for just about the whole day. No-one dived across the room, but the tears flowed freely. Tears of joy in celebration, but also tears of sadness that one so young had had this enormous task thrust upon her. How they admired her and that other Queen, Salote, who braved the elements and won the hearts of everybody.

Upstairs were three bedrooms, and a bathroom with lavatory. The water was heated by a boiler behind the fire, and the hanging rod had a third position if the water needed heating.

Ken hadn't been joking about the washing-up. He switched on the light, winced as he looked at the pile of dirty dishes, and decided that tomorrow would be a better

At a particularly exciting point in the game . . .

time to wash up and clean up. The fire was still in. He prodded it into life with the poker and added a few pieces of coal from the scuttle standing on the hearth. He put the kettle on the gas ring and made himself a mug of tea. The beer had given him an appetite, and so he made himself a ham sandwich.

He settled in the easy chair and rested his feet on the end of the mantelpiece. As he did so he glanced at the clock – eleven o'clock. The clock got him thinking. He rose to his feet and took it from the mantelpiece to look at it more closely. He then settled back in the chair with the clock still in his hands. Clocks had always seemed important in their family. Upstairs they had one which his mother's father had sent them. She treasured it. He'd won it in a leek competition. In fact he seemed to win lots of clocks through this pastime.

The clock Ken was holding was much smaller and simpler than the one upstairs. It had been carved from a piece of oak, rescued from the wreck of the *Ark Royal* by the ship's carpenter on the HMS *Benbow* – his father's ship in the First World War. Semi-circular in shape, its base measured about 9 inches wide, stood 6 inches high, and was 2 inches thick. The face had a diameter of 2 inches and the rest of the front was decorated by flowing, simple, leaf-like shapes. For years this clock had had no face or mechanism, and was kept in a cupboard. Then one day, four years ago, his father had a mechanism fitted and they had started to use it. Why he'd done this, Ken didn't know. He realized that there were lots of things about his parents he didn't know, but he felt that the sooner he did know, the better it would be. Perhaps now was the time to try and think it through. He hadn't to be up early the next morning, and he felt warm and comfortable – and still a little light-headed from the beer.

Ken learned about his father's wartime naval experiences, as a boy, mainly at mealtimes. He was totally absorbed by the stories from around the world. For example, how once when their ship had required urgent repairs, and a Russian port was the nearest available, the Russians had admitted them but had given them a very short time to get the work done and move out. His father had seen a lot of action, but had also missed a lot – because he happened to be a more than useful footballer, representing the Navy as a scheming inside-left (his father's term this) on several occasions. 'The Senior Service, The Royal Navy,' his father always referred, proudly, to it as. Apart from his four years as a sailor, and two years as a bookmaker's clerk, all Ken's father's working life had been spent as a coal-miner. On Ken's birth certificate his father's occupation was entered as 'Coal Miner (Hewer)'.

Ken's parents were 'Geordies', both from Blaydon-upon-Tyne, County Durham, and had had to move to Yorkshire in the early nineteen-twenties when work wasn't available in the pits in the north. During one period of unemployment, and before he was married, his father had obtained work as a bookmaker's clerk travelling the race-courses in the north of England and Scotland. He had known the bookmaker for many years as a customer, and the bookmaker had always been impressed by his grasp of arithmetic – mental and written – and was glad to take him on when the opportunity arose. Also, he had a fine tenor voice and could help with the entertainment in the evenings after the day's work. The bookmaker wanted him to stay with him, but when work returned in the pits his mother persuaded him to go back to his previous job. Bookmakers weren't regarded as being very respectable in those days.

Ken was an only child, and for many years it had looked as though the marriage would be childless. He had been born in a mining village, Millthorpe, in 1938, to a surprised and delighted couple. His father was by then forty years old and his mother thirty-five. They had moved to live at North Dene two years later when his father changed pits. Ken had always known this, but had never thought anything about it – not, that is, until the day of his father's funeral. Ken had only been to two funerals before his father's, because almost all his relatives still lived in the north. When grandparents, aunts, or uncles died, only his mother or father could afford to attend. Even so, Ken had noticed two things about funerals – that they could have a funny humorous side to them, and also that long-kept family secrets had a happy knack of spilling out into the open. His father's funeral had certainly conformed to this pattern.

His father's death had happened suddenly. The Capstan Full Strength cigarettes, his pipe, and the coal dust, had caught up with him. Nearing retirement, he had started having chest pains. These didn't prevent him working. But then, one day, at the end of a night-shift, he'd had a massive heart attack and was rushed to hospital from the pit. He died two hours after admission. His mother had coped better than Ken with his death, for after all she had already experienced deaths of her parents, brothers, sisters and friends in abundance. In fact his mother had often been called on to lay people out if someone had died in the vicinity – such was her knowledge and experience of these matters. Ken had missed his father tremendously in the first few months, but was finding that, if anything, he was missing him even more as time went on.

The day of the funeral was a fairly typical showery April one. Many relatives from Durham, old friends from Millthorpe, and neighbours at North Dene, made up the funeral party. As the hearse and following cars made their way up the street, the people of the street stood at their gates paying their last respects. Although his father never attended church, and his mother only occasionally – though she did support all the functions and fund-raising

. . . paying their last respects . . .

activities – his mother insisted that the coffin be taken into the church for a short service before proceeding to the cremation at Sheffield. The vicar of North Dene accompanied them. There wasn't a crematorium in Barnfield, and his mother was following his express wish that he be cremated, not buried. An aunt and uncle, who lived at Sheffield, were waiting for them when they arrived at the crematorium. One Sunday morning, during the war, Ken's father had walked all the ten miles to Sheffield to see if they were all right after a particularly heavy bombing raid the night before. Barnfield was never bombed, although 'Lord Haw Haw' had mentioned it in one of his broadcasts. He had told the Barnfield people that they hadn't been forgotten and that picks and shovels were going to be dropped on them so that they could dig themselves to death – no doubt a reference to the fact that coal mines were difficult to destroy by bombing.

After the funeral there were refreshments, which had been arranged at a public house in Barnfield. When these had been consumed, and a glass or two of beer drunk, the atmosphere began to lighten a little. The Royal Oak had an upstairs room used for such occasions, but now the party was downstairs in the lounge. Though the grief had been intense in the afternoon, life had to go on. Death was no stranger to these hardy mining folk, and although it was never welcome they were always well prepared. Their childhoods at the beginning of the century hadn't had antibiotics, vaccines, good sanitation, and the good housing enjoyed by Ken's generation. He looked around the room and realized that these were the survivors. He'd known them all for years, and so knew a lot about them and their histories. Histories related to him by his parents. They all had much in common. They were usually members of large families in which brothers and sisters had died in childhood or early youth.

They were reminiscing. It seemed to be the happier,

humorous events that were being recalled. Much of the humour centred on the Second World War, when the men had stayed at home because they were either too old for active service or else they were needed in the pits. Uncle Fred was entertaining everyone, relating his times spent as a fire-watcher – and funny they were. Most of them had something similar to tell, and so the stories multiplied. Ken listened happily. Having been born just after the outbreak of war, his memories of the war were totally different. He remembered the black-outs, the sirens, the air-raid shelters at the bottom of the gardens, the doodle-bugs, and home-made flags sticking out of every bedroom window in the street when the war was won. The bonfires and street parties – events which he'd never forget. They were exciting times for him. They remembered the food and clothes shortages, digging up the front lawn to plant potatoes – but tonight it mainly seemed to be fire-watching.

Later in the evening, Ken found himself sitting next to Percy Hooper – now a retired colliery deputy – who had moved to North Dene from Millthorpe before they had.

'Your dad started at Millthorpe at the same time as me,' said Percy.

'I didn't know that.'

'Yes, 1922. I remember when they came from Durham. I moved from Shotsfield pit to Millthorpe then.'

'Are you a Shotsfield man then, Mr Hooper?' asked Ken.

'Yes. Born and bred.'

'Why did you move to North Dene?'

'Got a better job. Managed to get a shot-firer's job at Bradstone and the travelling was too far from Millthorpe, so we moved house. The wife wasn't too keen, at first, because she had friends and relatives at Millthorpe. But she soon settled down. I helped your dad get a job at Bradstone, when he was victimized at Millthorpe.'

'Victimized?' said Ken, looking astonished.

Percy noticed Ken's reaction and went quiet.

Eventually he said, 'I thought you knew all about that Ken ... I just assumed you knew. Look, I'm sorry if I've upset you lad, I wish I'd never mentioned it, especially today. I'm sorry ... I'm sorry.'

'You've nothing to apologize for, Mr Hooper. Don't upset yourself. You haven't upset me. You haven't, really.'

'You looked upset.'

'More surprised than upset. That's all. How did you help him get the job?'

'Put a good word in for him with the manager. He'd worked under me at Millthorpe, so I knew what he was like.'

'That was good of you.'

'I always liked Ben.'

'Why was he victimized?'

'It's a long story, really. He got involved with the union, that I do know, and he did stir things up a bit. He could have a short fuse when he was younger, you know. To be fair though, a lot of what he said and argued for I agreed with. But we told him to be careful.'

'What form did this victimization take?'

'Times have changed, lad, in the pits, since those days. Then, certain people in the union – and they were usually the same people who had a lot of influence in the village – could decide who got the work. This didn't matter when the work was plentiful, but in the mid-nineteen-thirties there wasn't a lot to go round. Your dad was down to working one and two days a week – if he was lucky. He couldn't keep a house together on that.'

'Didn't the management have much say then?'

'They kept well out of such things. So long as the job got done, that's all that concerned them.'

At that point Mrs Hooper came across the room and

said it was time for them to be going to catch a bus home. She was a short, stocky, bustling woman, who seemed to be always laughing. When his mother and Ken had arrived back from the hospital, after his father had died, Ken had gone straight to the Hoopers to let them know. This had seemed just the natural thing to do. There were friends and neighbours in their street he could have gone to first, but without a second thought he'd gone to the Hoopers.

Ken looked at the clock, but was having difficulty putting victimization and his father together. He hadn't had a chance to ask Mr Hooper for more details, and hadn't asked his mother about it, not wishing to upset her in the wake of the funeral. But now, eighteen months on, it not only seemed necessary, to end his curiosity, but also to help him move forward. It had only dawned on him in this period what a strong-willed woman she was. Their arguments had been a clash of wills. Before, he could hardly ever remember an argument between them. He'd clashed more with his father, but even these were rare events. In fact arguments between his parents had been few and far between. Only two could he remember in any detail.

Once, in late Spring, his father won one hundred and fifty pounds on the football pools. The polished table, an electric washer, new curtains and other items usually out of reach were bought. Two weeks' holiday, not one, spent at Blackpool. The summer was a glorious one, but this caused the trouble. His father preferred the sun and going horse-racing to going to the pit. Ken was glad when the money ran low and his father returned to the pit on a regular basis. The rowing ceased.

The second concerned his mother's high blood pressure, which started when she was forty-eight. The doctor said that she must take things much steadier and have help with the washing and housework. His father worked regular nights at that time, and his first shift of the week was Monday. So he volunteered to help with the washing on

39

Monday mornings. He didn't have the necessary patience for the job. He wanted it doing in half the time it normally took, to his wife's great annoyance. Doing the washing kept him from his 'Bibles', as she called them. Before helping with the washing, Monday mornings and afternoons were mainly spent reading. He went back to bed after tea to prepare for the night shift. He would finish reading Sunday's *Reynold's News*, read Monday's *Daily Herald*, and then the 'Bibles'. The only ones Ken remembered were *Religion and the Rise of Capitalism* by Professor R.H. Tawney, *An Essay on Racial Tension* by Philip Mason, and *Thinking To Some Purpose*, by Susan Stebbing. They had quite a library in the front room. The problem was solved when a neighbour started doing most of the washing for a small payment, though this didn't last long once the blood pressure was under control.

On the whole, Ken could only find one word to describe his home life and his life at school and with his pals in the street – 'Idyllic'. But as with most such things, he hadn't realized this till later.

At North Dene his father had led a very simple life, in fact – he now realized – quite a solitary one. But he'd seemed quite content, so however could the man that he knew be 'victimized'? Ken was puzzled.

'Let's give him some thought,' Ken mused to himself. 'Look for clues.'

He knew that some neighbours had thought him a bit stern, and to outward appearances that had been the case. He had been friendly with them, but not close with any of them. His one close friend lived in Millthorpe – a Scotsman, Andrew Murdoch, a miner like himself, who had worked his way up to become an overman. Although Ken remembered nothing about living at Millthorpe, he knew Millthorpe very well. Because for as long as he could remember they had, occasionally, visited the Murdochs for Sunday tea, and vice versa. They had three children –

40

two girls and a boy – and they were like brothers and sisters for Ken. Some Christmasses were spent together at Millthorpe, others together at North Dene. Agnes Murdoch was also a Scot. They had both lived near Motherwell, met, married, and migrated south for work. Ken loved them all, and the happy times spent together – especially the evenings whiled away playing cards – Find the Lady, Rummy and Whist being their favourite games.

Ben Appleyard and Andrew Murdoch had three common interests: Sport (soccer and horse-racing principally), coal-mining (they were forever discussing the latest developments and innovations of the time), and education. These were the bonds that held them together. Both of them had seen and taken part in much sport and mining, but neither had had much education. They tried to educate themselves by reading and attending, together, the occasional lecture at Sheffield University.

In the year nineteen-fifty, tragedy broke the bonds. Andrew was killed by a roof-fall at Millthorpe pit. Seven others died in the same accident. A year later Agnes and the three children returned home to Scotland to be near her family. The two families kept in touch, but Ben Appleyard never developed another close friendship. His guiding light had gone. To Ken it had never seemed an equal partnership – his father had looked up to and admired Andrew too much for this to be the case.

Ben Appleyard might, at times, look stern. But what a warm emotional side he had, too. This was the side that Ken knew best. The playful fighting and rolling, on the home-made clippy rug in front of the fire, before going to school when young. The joy when Dante won the Derby in 1948. The tears on the day he had returned from Blaydon after attending his mother's funeral. On that day Ken had tactlessly asked him, soon after his return, if he'd heard the result of the Colchester United versus Manchester United cup-tie replay. He'd interrupted his father's

41

Ken loved the happy times spent together.

. . . tragedy broke the bonds.

account of the funeral to ask this. He received a clip around the ear, and the tears welled up in his father's eyes. Ken had been surprised at this, as he had on the few occasions he'd ever seen him get excited. Footballers could excite him. Tom Finney, Stanley Matthews and Duncan Edwards certainly did. They had to travel to Huddersfield to see them play, because Barnfield had never managed to get to the First Division. Singers too, such as Kathleen Ferrier, Marion Anderson, Paul Robeson and Josef Locke. Josef Locke he remembered because his father had seen him at Barnfield Theatre Royal, before he was famous, and had returned home that night very excited about an Irish tenor he'd just heard.

Ken's success at school had excited him too, but he had odd ways of showing it. On announcing, one tea-time, that he had come out top of the class at junior school, his father's comment had been, 'God help the bottom.'

'Ben, for goodness sake, give the lad some credit,' his mother protested.

'Aye, well done lad, well done. Keep it up,' was all he replied.

Each time Ken jumped an educational hurdle his father had been excited, and each time the pattern had been similar. A growing tension as examinations approached, an easing off once taken, and then the mounting tension waiting for the results. The eleven-plus examination result came by post. The school-teachers had told Ken's parents that there was nothing to worry about, but that didn't stop them worrying – especially as Ken had had a touch of diarrhoea on the day of the examination. Ken remembered his father's hand trembling as he opened the letter. The trembling stopped and a big beam appeared on his face as he read the letter's contents.

Once settled in at Barnfield Grammar School, and good consistent reports brought home, Ken did get a bit annoyed – because the only parts of the reports his father

44

... at Barnfield Theatre Royal, before he was famous ...

commented on were the odd not-so-good bits and never the good parts. Being unruly in religious education seemed worthy of comment, but not top in algebra or geometry. His mother did compensate though. 'He's very pleased really, but doesn't say much because he doesn't want you to get swollen-headed,' was a typical reply when Ken grumbled to her about the unfairness of it all. Looking back now, Ken could understand it. His father couldn't quite believe it was true and that it could last. But last it did, and once the three years at university were completed he was much more relaxed, although not enough for him to attend the graduation ceremony. He made excuses about not being able to afford a shift off work. Ken's aunt from Sheffield accompanied his mother to see him get his cap and gown.

Percy had mentioned union activities, and yet Ken could only remember him attending the occasional union meeting – perhaps once bitten, twice shy? They were Labour people, as were the majority of their neighbours, but they didn't talk much about politics. On election days, local and national, one house in the street was used as a committee room for the Conservatives. They had a car ferrying voters to and from the polling booth in the church hall. In the evening the women made good use of this facility, even though they had no intention of voting Conservative. Everyone found it amusing. Even the neighbours whose house and car was being so used.

Meetings that his father rarely missed were those of the British Legion. These were held on a Sunday morning in a working men's club at Bradstone – and as the buses didn't start running until midday this meant walking the two miles to Bradstone in all weathers.

Ken glanced down at the clock. It was now five minutes to midnight. He realized that in the last hour he hadn't made much, if any, progress. He decided to go to bed, making a mental note to himself that he really would have to ask his mother about these things.

. . . in the last hour he hadn't made much progress . . .

THE NEXT MORNING he awoke early. Thinking it was too soon to get up, he made a pot of tea, toasted two teacakes, and retired back to bed with the morning's newspaper. As was its custom on Saturday mornings this particular paper provided its readers, on the front page, with a massively-busted pin-up to gaze at.

'Bit early for that,' he muttered, and turned straight to the back page, to read about the game and see how their rivals had fared.

'Reds blunt Blades,' ran the imaginative headline. The gate hadn't been a good one and the chairman was quoted as saying that he thought the people of the town weren't pulling their weight and ought to support the team more. 'What's he expect with a team like that. We haven't had a good season for five years,' Ken thought. Eventually, working from the back, he arrived at the pin-up. In the next column was a photograph of the Prime Minister, Harold Wilson, once more arriving at or leaving (it was hard to tell) London Airport. 'Only a Tory rag would let him compete with that,' he thought to himself, as he scrutinized her figure. He didn't bother reading what the Premier was up to, put down the paper, and then had a quick bath and shave. As he dressed he organized the rest of the day. First, clear the mess downstairs. Second, hoover the carpet. Third, get some dinner and then set off in good time for the match.

The pots and the carpet were finished in an hour, and as he surveyed the scene he shook his head. It still didn't come up to scratch, but as he didn't know how to improve on it he left it and set off to the butcher's for two lamb chops. He enjoyed Saturday mornings if there was a game in the afternoon. He realized it was an escape of some kind, but an innocuous one that gave a lot of satisfaction. It was a bright sunny morning, with just a nip in the air to remind you that autumn was almost here. The fine morning had brought out plenty of early morning shoppers, and on his way back he met two other young chaps who played in the local leagues. They strolled along, kidding each other about their respective teams and discussing any interesting incidents that had come to light during the past week. The season was only a month old, but even so it was becoming apparent which teams were going to be grasping for honours later. Their teams were run-of-the-mill; therefore they decided that certain teams had an unfair advantage, as they poached all the best players with inducements such as free beer and travelling expenses. The result of this was that invariably the same players got most of the trophies year after year. They unanimously decided that a 'glory hunter' was the lowest form of local footballer.

He didn't bother laying the table, but sat with a plate on a stool in front of the television, watching the last few overs before lunch of the Gillette Cup Cricket Final at Lords. The meal over, he poured himself a glass of beer and lit a cigarette. On completion of the morning's play a recently-retired Test player perched himself in front of a camera and proceeded to pour forth platitudes which occasionally competed with the superlatives. He switched off, and set off for the match.

On the way he picked up two team-mates and arrived at the ground in good time.

'Put out the flags,' shouted Ray, as they entered.

'All here?' asked Ken.

'Yes. You're the last, even now!'

Filthy jokes, crude insinuations, atrocious language and assessments of the Scarsthorpe players mingled compatibly with the smell of liniment and mildly perspiring bodies.

They quickly changed and went out onto the field for a five-minute warm-up. Everybody was joking and moving about in order to lessen the tension that always exists before a game. No spectators were present, as the pubs had only just stopped drawing beer. The first half was quiet, with no goals being scored and neither team being able to dominate the other. The second half followed a similar pattern until, with only fifteen minutes left, the Scarsthorpe centre-half almost amputated, above the knee, Ray's right leg. The rule was that whoever was sinned against took the resultant penalty kick. Ray calmly stroked the ball into the net with the side of his left foot, thrust one arm into the air, collapsed, and was then carried off the field in triumph. Abuse poured from all sides of the field. Taking a throw-in became a risky affair. They held out, and left the field weary but happy.

'Great, lads,' said Ray, once they were back in the dressing-room. 'I think we just about deserved it.'

In the showers, the game's outstanding incidents were recollected from different angles, and good-humoured insults exchanged.

'Less beer and women on Friday nights and we'd have crucified 'em,' said one.

'Not enough of the second if you ask me,' said another.

'Hear, hear!' said Ray. 'It's alright for these married guys who've forgotten what it's like to fall asleep thinking about out-of-reach delectable females.'

'Haven't noticed them being out of reach as far as you're concerned,' came the reply.

'The delectable ones are, mate. When soaked with ale I can get my share of what's going – but, god, they look rough the next morning. The agony of trying to forget just ain't worth the fleeting joys of the night before.'

'Listen to the poet,' was the reply from a distant corner of the room.

'Let's have yer money,' the secretary interrupted. This

suggestion was greeted with a chorus of boos, Go to Hell's, and other well-intentioned remarks. To keep North Dene Football Club in existence each player had to pay a certain amount each week. Everyone was quite happy about the arrangement, but the Hon. Sec. had to put up with a weekly barrage of leg-pulling. Once the money had been collected they started to make their way home, leaving in ones and twos, all being reminded about next week's match. Ken and Ray were the last to leave, gathering the dirty tackle and balls together before doing so.

'Going by yourself?' asked Ray.

'Yes. Denis and Frank are going to the pictures with the girlfriends. They've dashed off.'

'I'll have a lift then, if you don't mind.'

'Sure. Jump in.'

Scarsthorpe was a mining village situated five miles out of town. It consisted of rows of stone terrace houses, slung up when the pit shaft was dropped during the early nineteen-twenties. Even now the roads between the houses were just rough cobblestones, made treacherous by the fact that the houses were built on a steep slope. It boasted one sparsely-attended chapel, two well-attended working men's clubs, and two public houses. Its one redeeming feature was the surrounding countryside. The home environment was utterly depressing, but on the doorstep were woods, fields and every enchantment a child could ask for. The pit was now in its death-throes, and the village had started to take on an added desolation. Many of the houses were unoccupied as some of the men, anticipating the shut-down, moved away in search of alternative employment. The only newcomers were people glad of cheap (if very poor) accommodation.

Ken pulled off the grass verge surrounding the field and moved off through the village in the direction of the town. One or two cars sat incongruously on the cobblestones.

'What a depressing hole,' said Ray.

'Hmm.' Ken replied. 'It's funny, isn't it, because most of the other pit villages around here have plenty of shops, a recreation ground, and are pleasant sorts of places.'

They sat in silence, without any tension or embarrassment. They had known each other for a long time now, and didn't feel the need to talk to each other just for the sake of it. As they reached the outskirts of the town, Ray broke the silence.

'Getting fed up with football, Ken?'

'I think I am a bit.'

'You don't seem as enthusiastic these days.'

'I'm not concentrating as I used to do. Probably ready for a rest.'

'Do you want us to pick you for next week?'

'I'm not available – we've got that cricket semi-final at Doncaster.'

'Going to the dance tonight?'

'Sure. Aren't you?'

'Never known me miss a beer and sex orgy, have you? Optimists eternally aren't we? Week after week we go to this dance, thinking that the sex will follow the beer, but it never does . . . or does it?' he asked, turning with a quizzical look at Ken.

'What's that supposed to mean? I'm as sex-starved as the next. Oh, I take one home occasionally, but that's as far as it goes.'

'Do you think Tony's doing owt for his barmaid, then?'

'Very likely. This once-bitten-twice-shy is all my arse. She's the type who had it early, decided it was better than jam and bread, and has made a meal of it ever since. I asked Tony himself and he didn't say yes or no, so you can draw your own conclusions. Let's face it, he's a randy sod.'

'He should be learning a bit, then.'

'Should be!'

By now they were well through town.

'Thanks a lot,' said Ray as they pulled up outside Ray's home. 'What time tonight?'

'About eight?'

'Downstairs in the bar first, then up to the dance around nine.'

'I may be late. My mother's coming back after tea. I've to pick her up and listen to the events of the past fortnight. I should make it for soon after eight. Cheerio then.'

'So long, see you later.'

4

IT WAS NOW half past five, and the train wasn't due till half past six. He set the things ready for tea and sank into an easy chair, propping his feet on the mantelpiece. He was tired, and felt as though he would soon fall asleep. 'Mustn't nod off, or else,' he said to himself. He splashed his face under the cold water tap and decided that he'd better set off now just in case the train should arrive early. 'These holiday excursions are unpredictable, so I'll be on the safe side,' he thought.

On arriving at the station he asked a porter, who was standing at the entrance, if the Rhyl train had arrived.

'You're early mate. Not due in for another twenty-five minutes or so. And I wouldn't bank on it then.'

'How have the excursions been running today?' asked Ken.

'Some early, some late,' he replied, glancing away as he did so in a manner that seemed to say he had things to concern himself with other than arrival times of trains.

'Thanks,' said Ken a little sarcastically, and walked along the platform. It was crowded with people who were waiting for trains to arrive, and also with holidaymakers returning from Blackpool. The public address system announced that the train which had just arrived was from Morecambe and Blackpool, and should have arrived at four o'clock.

'Sounds promising,' said Ken to a little hunched chap standing next to him.

'Huh!' he replied with a look of incomprehension on his face, not bothering to look in Ken's direction. The men, sweating profusely, were struggling along with suitcases in both hands, whilst the women were busily scolding their offspring for waving sand spades around in a fashion likely to decapitate the nearest thing in range. They were deeply suntanned, in contrast to the pale-faced relatives and friends who were waiting for them.

When the crowds started to thin he looked around for a seat. He noticed one at the end of the platform and made his way along, knocking his legs occasionally against somebody's suitcase when he wasn't quick enough to do a side-step. By the time he reached it the only space available was in the centre. It would mean squeezing himself between a youngish girl on one side and a rather plump middle-aged woman on the other. The seat was the last one, and his approach indicated his intentions. He hesitated, stroked his hand down his cheek, and was about to abandon the idea when the middle-aged woman looked up, smiled, and made a movement as if moving over to make room for him. The extra space so provided was only an inch or two.

She said cheerily, 'Room for a little 'un.'

Ken smiled weakly in reply.

'Thank you, but I'm not so little.'

'You're slim enough though,' she added.

He lowered himself slowly into the gap, attempting to avoid any contact if possible. The girl looked displeased and slightly embarrassed. She turned and stared away down the track. As he settled himself he knocked his arm against hers.

'Sorry,' he said.

There was no reply. The woman on his right was still beaming and he smiled at her once more, feeling that this was what she expected. This made her beam even more.

'Are you waiting for the Rhyl train?' she asked.

'Yes,' said Ken, looking straight ahead.

'It'll be late – always is,' she said.

'Will it?' he said automatically.

She then turned and started talking to the man next to her. It must have been her husband, for he didn't bother to say anything, listening expressionlessly and nodding from time to time. The conversation was about food, and whether she'd bought enough to last until Monday. She asked his advice, but didn't really expect any reply. She eventually persuaded herself that she had sufficient and that it was too bad if she hadn't.

Meanwhile, Ken had taken an early edition of the evening newspaper from his jacket pocket and was glancing at the front page. His attention was mainly occupied by the young girl on his left. She was now more at ease, sitting comfortably, leaning unavoidably with a little pressure against Ken's arm. He noticed that she had a well-shaped leg and a smooth, clear, complexion. She had medium brown hair which sat gently on her shoulders, so that when she turned it moved in the opposite direction to the turn and after a few to and fro movements came to rest in the original position. Ken concluded that she must be alone, because the woman sitting next to her was in deep conversation with a woman sitting at the end of the seat. Neither of them ever made reference to the girl or gave any indication that they were accompanying her. At one point he thought of saying something to her, but declined to do so. The ensuing silence which would inevitably follow would be awkward, he argued to himself, and left it at that.

A voice from the loudspeaker then announced, 'The Rhyl train is running early and will enter platform six, and not platform two as was announced earlier, in approximately five minutes time.'

This was repeated, but the voice was drowned by the noise of delighted expression at this news.

Everyone immediately made for the bridge which led to platform six. Ken didn't join the general rush, but ambled along slowly in the rear. The young girl had jumped up quickly and hurried along the platform. He watched her with a sensual satisfaction as she threaded her way through the crush. She had a graceful provocative walk,

Everyone immediately made for the bridge ...

her slim hips appearing to barely move beneath the cotton dress, her hair swinging jauntily from side to side. She was soon out of sight and lost in the crowd.

He was one of the last to reach the platform, and as he did so the train was drawing to a halt. Passengers were hanging out of the windows, hoping to recognize one of the waiting mass. When they did they waved excitedly and turned back into the carriage to inform the others that so and so was waiting for them. He remained stationary, knowing that his mother would wait until the crowd had dispersed a little before making an appearance, to attract Ken's attention. After about five minutes he looked up and noticed someone waving to him from the far end of the platform. The sun glared in his face and he couldn't be certain if the person was waving for him or not. He put his hand above his eyes as a shield and briskly marched towards the front of the train. He walked twenty yards or so, recognized that it was his mother, and ran to greet her.

He kissed her gently on the cheek and asked, 'You look well. Have you had a nice time?'

'Yes. Couldn't have been better. The weather was beautiful, in fact too hot at times,' she said, pointing at her face which was a ruddy brown and had small patches of flaking skin.

He smiled, and then went into the carriage to get the suitcase.

As they made their way to the car she started relating various details about the homeward journey – who had been in the carriage, where they lived, how many children they had, what she'd had to eat, which places they'd passed through etc. Ken didn't need to say anything, but listened with interest and mild amusement, watching the changing expressions of her face. When he was putting the case into the boot of the car she got around to asking him how he'd managed.

'Pretty well,' he said.

'You look pale. Have you been having proper meals?' she asked, looking at him admonishingly.

'I'm OK. Don't natter!' he replied, laughing as he slammed down the boot cover.

'Bet you haven't had a decent meal since I went away, have you?'

'I've been having a three course dinner at work and drinking plenty of beer, so I haven't come to any harm.'

'Drinking beer! What good do you think that will do you? You've been drinking too much recently.'

'Perhaps I've been having a little more than usual, but nothing excessive. Got to be sociable, you know,' he replied, pulling out onto the main road.

'Slow down, this hill's steep,' she said, clutching at the door handle.

'Mother, dear, I'm driving the car and will drive it as I think fit and not as you think I ought to do. As it happens, for your special benefit, I'm travelling at ten miles an hour less than I normally do when coming down here. Satisfied?' he said a little sharply.

'No, I'm not. I still think it's too fast,' she said, undeterred.'

The road levelled out and her hand relaxed its grip. Hills and speeds above forty miles an hour always made her nervous, and although he tried to avoid any clash on this account, he did, from time to time, have to stand these rebukes about his driving capabilities.

'Have you got anything in for the tea?' she asked.

'No. I've laid the table and there's enough bread, but nothing else. You said that you'd see to the food.'

'You'd better stop at the shop on the left in that case. I'll get some salad, a roast chicken and a cake. I can pop out later for the other things.'

After fifteen minutes she returned with a bag full to overflowing. Ken ran out to carry it.

'You've got a lot of salad or a big chicken,' he said as he

took the bag from her, buckling at the knees as if the weight was too much for him.

'Oh, I saw a few things we needed, so I thought I might as well get them.'

On entering the house he waited for the reaction. His mother didn't say anything. She casually looked round, smiled, and then asked, 'Who's cleaned up for you?'

'How do you mean? I spent two hours this morning getting it like this.'

She was obviously delighted, but didn't actually say so. This had the effect of putting her into a good mood. During tea he heard all about the things that had happened during the holiday. In the next hour, two of the neighbours called in to ask if she'd had a pleasant time. The suitcase had to be opened and the presents for the neighbours' children distributed. The children then came and shyly offered their thanks, making a hasty retreat to advertise to the other children in the street their new acquisitions. Children were attracted to his mother as though she was the Pied Piper of Hamelin. Apart from her friendliness they loved just listening to her speak – she hadn't lost her Newcastle accent even after all these years. Ken had settled in a chair with a novel, his time being evenly divided between reading and absorbing the events taking place in the room. At half past seven he got up to get changed for the dance.

'Going out?' his mother asked.

'Yes, I promised to meet Ray, so I must go.'

She didn't answer.

He quickly changed, had a run over with the electric razor, and shouted as he left, 'Don't wait up. I may be late.'

He arrived at the Imperial Hotel, where the dance was held, at five minutes past eight.

The suitcase had to be opened.

5

As he entered the lounge he looked around to see if Ray, and the rest of the crowd who congregated there every Saturday night, had arrived. The place was already almost full, all the seats being taken and a knot of people standing at the bar. He noticed them sitting in one of the recesses at the far end of the room. Their beer glasses were out of sight from where he was standing and he made a miming action at Ray, asking if they were ready for refills. In reply Ray held up his glass, which was three quarters full. Ken nodded. There was only one barmaid, and he had to wait a few minutes before getting served. He ordered a pint of best and remarked to her that she ought to be paid at the double-time rate on nights like these. He gave her the money and asked her to have something. She was an elderly lady who had been the barmaid there for as long as Ken and his friends had been frequenting the place. They all liked her and appreciated the pleasant service that they always received. If they asked her to have a drink she only accepted if she felt like having one and hadn't already got one from someone else. On this occasion she answered that she'd just started a glass of bitter and thanked him anyway. The space between the tables was such that it was a tricky manœuvre getting to the recess without pouring beer over someone. After spilling a little on the carpet he arrived without mishap at the table. They moved along the bench seat to make room for him.

'Not too late after all,' said Ray.

'The train was early,' he replied, turning as he did so in Tony's direction. 'Surprised to see you here, tonight, Tony,' he said, smiling.

'I'm a freelance,' was the reply. The others in the

company looked puzzled.

'What's all this about?' one of them asked.

'Oh, nothing,' Ken replied.

'Any talent shown up, yet?' he continued, abruptly changing the subject. He suspected that Tony might be displeased at him for having alluded, even indirectly, to his relationship with the barmaid.

'Haven't seen anything special,' Ray replied, quick to notice what Ken was probably thinking.

The conversation continued quietly, each one busily engaged with his neighbour, talking about common interests and developing, in some cases, a topic that had been brought up the previous week. Saturday night had an entirely different tempo to that of Friday night. This bar was almost exclusively used by professional and business people, and if someone unfamiliar with this happened to enter, and if he also happened not to belong to this class, he soon retreated after one drink, or sometimes not even bothering to have a drink. So the general atmosphere of the place was sober, imposing itself on their company. It served as the perfect appetizer.

They each had another two pints before going upstairs to the dance. By now all the tickets would be sold, but as they had an arrangement with the man at the door this presented no difficulties. The admission price was six shillings, and entrance was by ticket only. If one of them had been in town during the day he'd buy half a dozen tickets, and if not they surreptitiously gave Fred a couple of shillings and walked in. Fred gave them a warning by shaking his head from side to side as they reached the top of the stairs. This indicated that the manager was in the near vicinity. Therefore they slipped into the toilet which served the downstairs bars and also the dance patrons. A pass-out ticket had to be obtained if nature called. After a wash and tidy up they tried again. This time Fred beckoned them on. They each made as if to be giving him a ticket and passed him a two shilling or half-crown piece. It was risky, and they made a point of not abusing the facility.

Immediately beyond the entrance was the bar which, although a good size, usually proved to be inadequate. Tonight was no exception. When they entered the band was silent, and so the bar was unapproachable, being completely surrounded.

'Are we having one, before going on the prowl?' asked Ray.

Two of them replied that they'd had enough for now and intended having a look around. Ken and Tony decided they could manage one. Ray, without much inhibition, pushed his way through to the bar, and soon reappeared with three half-pints.

'Sorry about the half pints, but apparently they're only going to serve half-pints from now on. Manager thinks it looks better.'

'A big pint pot lowers the tone of the joint.'

'Makes more work,' said Tony.

'Can't you tell he's joined the Barmaid's Protection Union,' said Ken.

They laughed.

Most of the people present were aged between twenty and thirty. The teenagers of the town were catered for elsewhere, and wouldn't entertain the music and type of dancing offered here, anyway. The atmosphere was lively and the girls always well turned out. As they sipped at the beer they were taking in the whole scene, noticing which of the regulars were present and if any newcomers had joined the ranks. Several people said 'Hello' as they passed, and one or two of them, whom they knew better, stopped to talk for a while. The dance floor itself was in a room adjacent to the bar and only light refreshments were allowed in there.

Ray situated himself at the entrance to view who was

present. Talking back over his shoulder, he said, 'Looks most promising tonight – most promising!'

'New faces?' asked Tony.

'H'mm, pretty ones too. Mustn't have any more beer after this one. Got any peppermints, Ken?'

'Sorry. Ask Fred. He can usually oblige.'

'Ray went to the bar, got a glass of bitter, gave it to Fred and procured a peppermint. The band leader announced the next dance as a waltz, and started playing the latest pop tune that could best be adapted to the waltz tempo.

Emptying his glass at one gulp, Ray proceeded into the hall.

'Coming?' he asked Ken and Tony.

'In a minute,' they replied.

'You'll be too late.'

'That's what you say every week, and you never fare any better than we do,' replied Tony.

'It'll all be different tonight,' he replied, easing his jacket slightly by the lapels and touching his tie.

'Go on you vain devil; you look beautiful enough,' shouted Ken, as he joined the bunch of men standing at the entrance.

'Eager tonight, isn't he?' said Tony.

'Obviously seen something he fancies,' replied Ken.

They were joined by a colleague of Tony's, and stood chatting at the entrance before going in.

'Do you think you'll have a dance?' asked Ken.

'Oh, I'll have a dance, but I think that's about as far as I'll go. Our mutual friend Jean's here, so I'll be alright for a squeeze and a cuddle when the next waltz comes around. What about you?'

'Yes, I'm in the mood for it, if anybody else is. Dancing, I mean,' he added, smiling.

'Of course, what else?' replied Tony, putting on an innocent expression.

'Trouble is, so many of them are fussy and refuse to

65

dance,' Ken continued.

'What do you say to them when they say no?' asked Tony.

'I just say "OK. Thanks anyway." What do you say?'

'Depends how I'm feeling. Normally I walk away nonchalantly, but now and again I say, "Made a mistake anyway, thought you were somebody else; glad you said no".'

'Get on. You never say that!'

'True. Why shouldn't I say what I think? Obviously, if I like the girl I don't say that – otherwise I couldn't ask her again. They're nice,' he said, as they walked past two girls sitting on the seats nearest to the band. 'Fancy a try?' he continued.

'No, you go ahead if you wish.'

Tony walked up and asked one if she'd like to dance. She said 'Thank you,' and took his hand. As he moved into the first steps he raised his eyebrows at Ken and then started talking to his new partner.

'Come on, what's the matter with you?' a voice shouted at Ken as he proceeded in front of the band.

He turned, and saw Ray dancing with a short well-made girl.

'Plenty of time,' replied Ken, having a good look at Ray's partner. He looked her up and down, and thought, 'Always goes for the same type, does Ray. Fresh and buxom.'

Ray did a half turn so that he faced him, and the expression on his face asked, 'Well, what do you think?'

Ken pursed his lips and nodded his approval. He had a few words with the band leader, whom he knew quite well by virtue of his regular visits, and then sat down. He enjoyed listening to the music and watching the swirling skirts. After about half an hour he was joined by Ray.

'Had a dance yet?'

'No, but you're doing alright for yourself.'

'I might be in there. She's gone to powder her nose and then I'm going to buy her a drink. She's had one or two already, so if I get her another two she'll probably let me take her home.'

'What's she like?'

'Fine. Not shy, easy to talk to, snuggles up close.'

'What does she do?'

'Haven't discovered, so far. I'm in the process of finding out. I've eliminated hairdressing. She was disgusted when I suggested that. Nursing, teaching, physiotherapist, secretary – any ideas?'

'How does she speak?'

'Very well. Doesn't sound Yorkshire at all.'

'You've suggested all the obvious things. Try social worker. They usually speak rather nicely.'

'I'll tell her you suggested it if it's wrong.'

'Here she comes. She looks terribly organizational. Five bob she's a social worker.'

'You're on!' said Ray, and walked across to meet her. He took her by the hand and came up to Ken, saying, 'Pat, this is a friend of mine, Ken.'

She said 'Hello' as they shook hands.

'He says you go around being a fairy godmother to people in need.'

At this she burst into laughter.

'Heaven forbid,' she said.

'That's five bob you owe me, old son. Come on, let's have a drink before the bar closes. See you later Ken.'

'Bye,' said Pat, waving her hand as she left.

'Bye.'

Ken bought himself a cup of coffee and a ham sandwich, and sat talking to the woman behind the counter.

'You look fed up tonight Ken. Not your usual active self,' she said.

'I'm alright. I don't feel like dancing at the moment. I'm happy watching.'

'It's been a busy night.'

'Has it?'

'It's a pity it's not a bigger place. We turn a lot away every week.'

'Really.'

'That friend of yours is a warm lad, I'll say,' she said, smiling.

'Ray, you mean?'

'The plump one.'

'Yes, that's Ray.'

'Teacher, is he?'

'Yes.'

'Thought so. Looks a rough diamond. The kids'll love him.'

'I think they do.'

The band started playing again, and the floor was quickly crowded for a samba.

'This is about my pace tonight. I'll have a look what's available.'

'Some pretty girls here tonight.'

'Yes, I've noticed. Cheerio then.'

'Cheerio.'

Moving away, he bumped into Tony.

'I've been looking for you. Where've you been?'

'Had a coffee and a sandwich. Why?'

'Thought you'd like another drink before close down. Didn't like to go alone.'

'Wouldn't say no. How did you get on?'

'Nice enough. A bit too naive though.'

'Would you like a short?'

'Gin and tonic, preferably.'

'Two gin and tonics please,' he asked the barman.

The bar was empty now, and they sat on the stools provided.

The barmen were beginning to clear away the empty glasses. There were still a few couples sitting at the tables, but the majority were dancing. All the unattached men were competing for the few remaining non-dancing women.

'Seeing Mary tonight?' asked Ken.

'No. It will be too late. I'll go and make my peace tomorrow lunchtime. I'll have a drink and dry a few glasses. I think I'll have a dance for the last half hour. Come on.'

They left the bar and went into the dance.

'I think I'll ask this young lady here,' Ken said, looking towards a girl who was standing with her back to them.

'All the best,' said Tony.

Ken approached her, caught her elbow with his hand, and asked if she'd like to dance. She turned quickly to see who it was. It was the girl he'd seen in the station. She was a little non-plussed, and coloured as she looked into Ken's eyes. Lowering her eyes she didn't answer. He felt lost for what to do. He was embarrassed, and thought that it probably showed. After a few seconds he spluttered out, 'Well, would you?' and smiled at her.

She raised her eyes momentarily and replied, 'Yes, thank you,' a barely perceptible smile forming on her face.

As he held her he could feel how tense she was. He looked down at her but she kept her eyes averted. She moved easily, and when they accidentally bumped into someone he took the opportunity to pull her gently closer to him. She must have noticed, he thought, but she didn't resist.

The floor was now so crowded that dancing was almost impossible. He looked down at her again, and this time she returned his smile with a shy smile of her own. He didn't feel the need to say anything. At this time there were no intervals between the dances.

When the music changed from waltz to foxtrot he asked, 'Shall we stay on?'

69

She nodded. Now the tension was completely eliminated.

Eventually he said to her, 'Who were you waiting for this afternoon, if it isn't too personal?'

'My parents and young brother,' she replied softly.

'I didn't see you after you left for the other platform. Were they on that train?'

'Yes. I saw you again, putting a case into the boot of a car. We were walking by as you were doing it.'

'You'd see my mother then?'

'I did see a lady getting into the car.'

'You looked annoyed when I sat down.'

'I didn't think there was enough room, and thought that you'd probably crease my dress.'

'I wasn't going to sit down, but that woman insisted.'

'I was furious with her,' she said, laughing.

'You don't look as though you get furious,' he teased her.

'You don't know me,' she replied.

They completed two more circuits of the floor, and then the last waltz was announced. It was less crowded as people made off to get their coats and avoid having to queue at the cloakroom.

'Where do you live?' he asked.

'Burnside.'

'That's a fair journey. How do you get home?'

'I catch the special bus.'

'But it goes on a circular tour before getting there.'

'It's dreary. I don't get home till one o'clock.'

'I'll give you a lift if you wish.'

'That's kind of you. It's not out of your way, is it?'

'Wouldn't make any difference if it was,' he replied, evading the question.

'Shall we go now and save waiting for my coat?'

'Suits me. I'll wait in here for you. It's too crowded in there,' he said, pointing towards the bar.

70

She picked up her handbag from underneath the chair where she'd left it, and went through into the cloakroom. Ken sat down and looked around for Ray and Tony. He saw Tony sitting further up the room and moved to sit with him.

'How's Ray getting home?' Ken asked.

'He's gone. Got his father's car,' he replied. 'She looked very nice.'

'I'm taking home the one you saw me with.'

'Where's she live?'

'Burnside.'

'You must be bonkers. You've got half an hour's run home from there.'

'Who's bothered about that? What are you waiting for?' he asked.

Tony didn't reply.

'You're not taking Jean home?' he continued as the reason for Tony's silence dawned on him.

'Well,' he said, shrugging his shoulders, 'she hadn't got a lift, so I offered to oblige,' looking sheepish, then grinning all over his face.'

'I don't know how you stand the pace.'

'Steak three times a day,' was Tony's reply.

'I'd need intravenous glucose, as well,' said Ken, getting up as she peered around the door looking for him. 'Might see you tomorrow, so long.'

'Possibly, so long.'

6

HE TOOK HER ARM and escorted her down the stairs, receiving envious nods and the odd suggestive comment from acquaintances. The car was parked in the street outside. He opened the passenger door first, and held it open whilst she got in. As he went around to the driving side he encountered a policeman, who reminded him that, strictly speaking, he shouldn't park in this street. He put on an innocent expression, said he wasn't aware of that, and certainly wouldn't do so again. He'd said this to a different policeman for each of the last six weeks. When in the car he pulled out the choke, revved up, and set off with a sharp acceleration, jolting her head back. He hadn't had the car very long, and still tended to show off. She made a remark about reckless drivers.

Burnside was a small village, ten miles from Barnfield. To get there involved a journey through five or six miles of countryside. Once the town traffic had been negotiated he leaned back and relaxed. She slipped off her shoes and curled up, sitting on her feet. She'd already removed her coat as she entered the car, and her dress was now an inch or so above her knees. She let her head rest on the back of the seat, closing her eyes.

He asked her if she wanted the heater on.

'No, I'm nice and warm,' she replied.

He glanced at her, and then quickly away. Turning off the main road onto the minor road to the village he said, looking at his watch, 'It isn't twelve yet, and if you won't be expected till one shall we go for a drive?'

'Wherever you like,' she answered, 'on one condition.'

'And what's that?' he asked.

'You don't seduce me!'

'I used to be a boy scout, so you're OK.'

'They're the worst.'

Her eyes were still closed. Although she'd been receptive when dancing, he wasn't prepared for this. He slowed down and gazed at her. Sensing that he was looking at her she kept in the same pose and then, after a few seconds, opened her eyes, smiling at him, unblinking.

Regaining his composure he gave his attention to the road and said, 'Why, don't you want to be?'

She didn't answer. He started humming and she made herself more comfortable, once more closing her eyes.

'I'll turn off here,' he said, 'and go past the reservoir towards Burton church. Once up there there's a beautiful view of the valley.'

They sat in silence till they reached the church. He pulled onto the grass verge at the side of the church gate and switched off the engine. He sat back, breathing deeply. The only other buildings nearby were a derelict farmhouse and two or three small cottages, inhabited by farm labourers. The vicarage was in the next village, and services were only held here once a month.

'I like it up here,' said Ken. 'The tranquillity soothes.'

The moon was out and they sat looking out over the valley. He slipped his arm around her shoulders and she rested her head on his chest.

After a few moments she said, 'Let's go for a walk, shall we?'

He helped her on with her coat. They walked along the narrow road, arm in arm. The only noises to be heard were those of the leaves being rustled by the wind. When they arrived at a five bar gate, they stopped to look into the field. He stood behind, gripping her tightly about the waist, pressing himself against her. Lowering his head he kissed her on the side of the neck. She shivered. They remained at the gate a few moments before walking on, stopping in the middle of the road. He turned her to him and, drawing her close, kissed her. She felt warm and fragrant. She responded fully, putting her arms around him and arching herself so that she fitted snugly up to him.

'You feel gorgeous,' he said.

'Hmm,' she purred.

She was trembling slightly, and he increased the pressure of the kiss. He released his grip a little and walked her slowly backwards to a high wall which ran down the side of the road. There were trees in front of it, but room to pass between them. She leant against the wall, behind one of the trees.

'Don't forget what I said earlier,' she said smiling, twinkling her eyes at him.

'I haven't forgotten,' he replied. 'Scouts honour. Man of honour. I didn't seduce you, as requested,' he said as they sauntered slowly back to the car, peaceful and contented.

'Not far off though,' she replied, slapping his face in mock anger.

They flopped into the seats and sat for several minutes before driving off. She was smiling to herself. He noticed from the corner of his eye, and asked what the mirth was for.'

'Do you realize,' she said, 'you don't even know my name.'

'Sexy Susan,' he replied, resting his left hand on her knee, tickling it as he did so.

She laughed out loud, and then pretended to be very annoyed at this suggestion. She pulled her leg away from him, leaving his hand dangling at the side of the gear-stick. He left it there and then casually replaced it on her knee. This time she didn't move.

By a process of elimination he discovered that she was called Sandra and worked as a typist for a solicitor in town. Her father had a milk round and a smallholding, rearing hens and pigs. He had been a miner, but had had to retire prematurely because of dust on the chest. He'd

They sat for several minutes before driving off.

always had a yearning for the outdoor life. Now, with a disability pension, he was able to lead a life of his own choosing. She talked away happily about her background, and it was easy to tell that she had a contented home environment. Ken felt a little envious as she described her typical week. So simple and uncomplicated, he thought.

'Who did the milk round whilst your father was on holiday?' he asked.

'Oh, that's why it doesn't matter much what time I get in tonight,' she replied. 'I've been up at five o'clock during the last week, and taken the milk before going to work.'

'You must be all in.'

'Not really. All that walking early in the morning brings you alive.'

'Have you been cleaning the pigsties, too?' he asked, looking in her direction and sniffing.

'Cheeky blighter,' she laughed. 'No, dad has a friend who sees to them when he's away or ill.'

'Does he have much trouble with his chest?'

'Not in summer. He has to watch himself in winter, otherwise he soon catches pneumonia. He's had two bad attacks, frightening us stiff. He's so stubborn; insists on doing all his chores, even in the foulest weather. He now realizes that it's not worth it and mum asks his friend to do it if he's over-tired or if it's foggy and damp. He gets free milk and is glad to help out.'

'He won't be very old to have that complaint,' said Ken.

'Only forty-five. The first ten years in the pits he worked under atrocious conditions.'

'I suppose he has to take tablets permanently?'

'He takes a yellow one three times a day and he has some others which he lets dissolve slowly underneath his tongue, whenever his chest tightens. He makes a proper ritual of his pill-taking. Mum puts them out at meal times and makes sure he doesn't miss. The pills are for bronchitis, not to clear the dust.'

76

'It won't shorten his life much if he watches himself, will it?' he asked.

'The doctors say not, but they only tell him what he wants to hear. There are men in the village who've lived for years after leaving the pits with this trouble.'

'You want to go and live in the south of France. This climate can't help him.'

'Dad'd never leave Burnside. Born and bred and all that. Talking of the south of France, I'm going to Spain for my holidays in a month's time.'

He looked at her, surprised.

She continued, 'Four of us, out of the office. We've been saving like mad since last September.'

'Flying?'

'Yes, from Manchester. I'll be petrified.'

'Nothing to it,' said Ken.

'Have you ever flown?' she asked.

'No!' he said, laughing. 'Thought I'd say that to give you confidence.'

She playfully ruffled his hair and put her arm around his neck.

'Those amorous Spaniards will seduce you, given half a chance.'

'Oh, no they won't,' she replied.

'Two glasses of wine, and you'll tumble into bed without being asked.'

'That's what you think.'

'All the same, English girls on holiday. They protect their virginity to the point of insanity at home and, once abroad with a touch of the sun, they give it away like a Jehovah's Witness dishing out his pamphlets.'

'I'm the exception to the rule,' she replied, cocking her nose in the air.

'You mean you're not a virgin?'

She thumped him with both hands, on his shoulder and back.

'That little show of tantrums definitely proves that you're not.'

She put on a hurt look and folded her arms in front of her.

'Nothing to say?' he asked.

She didn't answer. He stopped the car and kissed her.

'Now,' he said as they entered the village. 'Which way?'

'Go straight through. Turn left at the fork as you pass the monument. Ours is the third cottage on the right.'

'We've played your team at football,' he said.

'Ugh!' she said. 'That set of roughnecks. I don't bother with them.'

'Here we are,' he said, pulling up alongside the house.

'They're all in bed,' she said. 'Sit quietly and you'll see the upstairs right curtain move. Mum won't be asleep, and hearing a car pull up she won't be able to resist having a peep.'

Sure enough, the curtain was drawn a little to one side and then quickly replaced.

Ken smiled and said, 'I'd better be off, in that case, or she'll be after me.'

'You can come in and have coffee.'

'No. I'd better not, thanks, it's getting late.'

'Sure?'

'Positive, thanks.'

'Thank you for the lift home, and . . . ,' she hesitated.

'And what?' he said, quickly.

She slapped him, blushing a little.

'Shall I be seeing you again?' he asked.

'If you wish.'

'Wednesday alright?'

She studied, and then said, 'Hmm.'

'I can pick you up here if you'd like me to.'

'Yes, please. I don't get home from work till half past six, and it's a rush getting back into town. I still don't know your name,' she said.

'I told you earlier,' he said, tapping his fingers against his lips.

'It'll sound fine tomorrow morning at breakfast,' she replied. 'Mother will say, "What's his name?" I will reply, "Rasputin." Dad will say, "He was a bloody Russian monk." Mum will say, "What does he do?" I will say, "Rapes unsuspecting spinsters." '

Ken couldn't stop himself from laughing. When he'd stopped, he said, 'My name's Ken, and I'm a chemist at the glassworks. Satisfied?'

'Thank you, that will sound better.'

He opened the car door, kissed her on the cheek, and said, 'Bye for now. I'll call about half past seven, Wednesday.'

'Bye,' she said, opening the gate. She waved to him when she reached the door. He waved back and revved the engine. She went inside and waved again as he set off for home.

The effects of the alcohol had worn off, and he had difficulty in keeping his eyes open. He drove quickly, cutting corner after corner. This was safe enough, as the hedges were low and he could see if anything was coming in the opposite direction a mile or so before meeting. He had to wait at a set of traffic lights in town. There was no traffic about, and they stayed at red for a long time. Impatiently he backed so that he could pass over the rubber again. As he did so the lights changed. He accelerated along the one way streets, slowing if he saw a policeman in a shop doorway. A young lad was standing outside a cinema with his arm outstretched, his thumb in the air. Ken stopped, stamping hard on the brake pedal, causing a screeching sound. He pushed open the door.

The lad asked, 'Going anywhere near Kidderton?'

'I live near there,' replied Ken.

'That's lucky,' he said, and jumped in. 'I missed the last bus,' he continued.

Ken looked at his watch and said, grinning at him, 'By about three hours, I would say.'

He didn't reply. Ken noticed that he was a good looking lad, neatly dressed, his hair long and wavy – probably between seventeen or eighteen years old. The type the young girls would go for in a big way, he thought.

To try and make conversation the lad said, mopping his brow, 'It's warm.'

'H'mm,' Ken replied, more intent on getting home quickly than talking. On a straight flat stretch he asked him, 'Been dancing?'

'Yes.'

'At the Locarno?'

'Yes.'

'Crowded?'

'Packed out!'

'Where does your girlfriend live?'

'Cornwood.'

Ken grimaced. 'You need your own transport to be going with someone there.'

'It's the first time and probably the last,' he replied. 'My dad'll kill me if he gets to know what time I get in.'

'Have you a key?'

'No. I can throw a stone at the window and my mother will let me in. I only hope it doesn't wake Dad. He has a drink on Saturday, so I'm hoping he's fast on.'

'Was it worth all this trouble?'

'Was it heck. It won't happen again.'

'You'll think differently by the time next weekend comes around.'

They didn't say anything more until Ken reached the turning into the estate.

'This OK for you?'

'Yes, thanks very much. I live in the road next to the pub.'

As he got out he tried to push a two shilling piece into

Ken's hand.

'No. No. No. I don't want that,' he said. 'I used to do the same thing myself when I was your age.' He made him take the money back and said, 'Goodnight.'

The street lights were out as he turned into the garage. He felt exhausted. He opened the door and went straight upstairs.

'That you Ken?' his mother's voice asked from her bedroom.

'Yes, it's me!'

'What time is it?'

'Half past twelve,' he replied, instantly. He then looked at his watch. It was half-past one.

'Goodnight,' he shouted.

'Goodnight. You locked the door?' she asked as an afterthought.

'Yes.'

He undressed, didn't bother putting on his pyjamas, and fell into bed.

7

THE NEXT MORNING he could hear somebody shouting him, but wasn't able to answer. It was as though he'd been struck dumb. After a few more shouts he managed to move the sheets back and he recognized his mother's voice. She asked him if he was ready for his breakfast. The alarm clock said nine o'clock, so he thought he'd better have it or otherwise he wouldn't get any as the dinner would soon be in preparation.

'I'll have it in bed, but I'll come down and collect it,' he replied, pulling the sheets back into place and sinking his head into the pillow. The next thing he knew she was standing at the side of the bed, with a tray in one hand, shaking him with the other.

'I've been calling you to come and get it for five minutes,' she said.

He yawned and looked up, screwing his eyes. The curtains were wide open, the sun flooding the room with light.

'Close the curtains, there's a dear,' he said.

'Have your breakfast and get yourself out of bed,' she replied.

He looked on the dressing table for cigarettes.

'Eat your food before poisoning your system with those things,' came the reply. He found the packet under a handkerchief, took one out, and lit it. His mother put the tray on a stool and went back downstairs without disguising her disgust.

'You haven't brought the papers,' he called.

'The lawn needs cutting,' was the reply.

He ate the breakfast and drank the tea. His head was still heavy and he went downstairs to get another cup. His mother was busily engaged in tidying the kitchen, and didn't take any notice of him. He looked around but couldn't see the papers anywhere and assumed they must still be in the letter-box. He found them lying on the floor in the lobby, and then returned to bed.

'I'll have a read for an hour, then see to the garden,' he said. 'Remind me when it's half past ten.'

At a quarter past ten he was reminded that it was half past. He hadn't found much to interest him in the papers, and was reading one of the latest best-selling paperbacks. So far it had been full of incest, drug addiction and doubt-ful family relationships. He closed it, saying to himself, '... don't think I'll read any more of that rubbish.'

He quickly washed and dressed in the oldest clothes he could find. As he went downstairs he caught the odour of coffee.

'Made me a cup?' he asked as he entered the living room.

There were two full cups on the table. He had another cigarette with the coffee and glanced through an article in one of the more popular newspapers about the sensational goings on in the tropical backwoods of Outer Mongolia.

'What time will dinner be ready?' he asked.

'Later than usual. Two o'clockish. I want to clean upstairs this morning.'

Cutting the grass was a fortnightly occurrence. It used to be weekly, but that had become irksome and he now alternated it with the privet hedge. Gardening wasn't something he had much interest in, but he didn't like to see things untidy.

He did the heavy work such as digging and mowing, his mother supplying the fine arts of flower growing and suggesting a new layout from time to time. After greasing the wheels he set to work. It was another hot, humid, day, and he was soon sweating profusely. He tended to rush at the start to get it finished quickly. With half of it done he sat on the wall and chatted to the chaps on either side who also spent Sunday mornings in the garden. He listened to the best way to grow a particular variety of rose, and their ideas on the newest model of car that had just been released.

'Back to it,' he said, 'Must leave time to have a quick one before dinner.'

They laughed at this. They didn't drink themselves, and were always amused by Ken's reference to going to the pub. He got the impression that they felt a little superior because they didn't go for a drink. Ken didn't see it this way and he wasn't affected by what they might be thinking. His mother was forever telling him not to advertise it too much. He soon finished, dismantled the mower, and replaced it in the shed. When he had done so his mother came to the door and said that as it hadn't taken long he might trim the side hedge.

'Haven't time,' he replied. 'Said I'd have a glass with Tony.'

'She looked displeased and said, 'I hope you'll be getting changed.'

'No,' he replied.

He was wearing a check shirt, badly frayed at the cuffs, khaki-coloured denims, and sandals.

'They're clean, if not elegant,' he continued, looking himself up and down.

'Well, at least put on a pair of socks.'

'Suppose I ought,' he replied, 'but I'm only going in the rough end.'

His mother went back into the house and threw a pair of socks out through the window.

'Thanks,' he shouted. 'Can you let me have ten bob till I get some change?'

'No. I can't.'

'Go on, I forgot to go to the bank yesterday.'

She handed him a pound note and said, 'Make sure you find time to go tomorrow, otherwise I'll be short later in

84

the week.'

'Thanks. Yes, I've to go into town at lunchtime tomorrow. I'll call then.'

He walked up the street, making a passing comment to anyone he happened to see. One or two of them made as if they wanted to stand and talk, but he kept on walking, trying to say something appropriate as he did so.

The pub had been open for half an hour, and it was fairly crowded. Tony and Ray, playing darts, nodded to him, and he ordered three pints. He took them over to the table nearest the dartboard and sat down. They were both well-dressed in dark suits.

'What's all this in aid of?' he asked, moving his eyes over them.

'Do you know this scruff who's just come in?' Ray said to Tony.

'Looks familiar,' replied Tony, 'but I can't put a name to the species.'

Ken had a long drink and said, 'Come on. I'm burning with curiosity. I haven't seen you two like this on a Sunday lunchtime since last Whitsuntide, when you went about showing everybody your new suits.'

'Very funny,' they replied.

'I'm taking Mary out to lunch. We're going to that new country club. It's posh, they say.'

'And I've been to church,' said Ray.

'This is the only church you go to,' replied Ken. 'Seriously though, have you been to church?'

'Yes. After last night I thought I'd better go and have my sins forgiven.'

'So good, was it?' said Tony.

'You're joking,' Ray replied.

'Met your match Ray?' asked Ken.

'She's delightful company, but you'll have to marry that one to get anything there.'

'You won't be seeing her again in that case,' said Ken.

85

Ray thought for a few moments . . .

'Having tea with her today, actually. She lives in a flat with a girl friend who's gone home for the weekend. I've been invited to tea – or rather I invited myself.'

'Nice work!' said Tony.

'What does she do then?' asked Ken.

'Still don't know. I suggested everything without getting it.'

'Probably a high class prostitute,' suggested Tony, laughing.

'Could be at that,' Ray replied. 'She has a car, and the flat is one of those new luxury types in Westbridge Road.'

'Whereabouts does she come from?' asked Tony.

'She's secretive about that as well. Speaks without an accent, so there's no clue there.'

'Sounds like Mata Hari's daughter,' said Ken.

'I bet she can perform like Mata Hari when she wants to,' replied Ray.

'I noticed she'd got the figure for it,' said Tony.

'Keep your eyes off mate,' said Ray.

'Guess who this one took home last night,' said Ken, nodding at Tony.

Ray thought for a few moments, standing poised to throw a dart, then said, 'Not Jean?'

They both laughed.

'Quiet,' said Tony, looking towards the bar. 'Jean's alright,' he continued softly.

'Trouble is, five thousand other blokes in the town know the same thing,' said Ray.

'She's not quite so bad,' replied Tony.

'That's what you think,' Ray answered. 'I hear that you did alright for yourself, Ken?' he continued.

'No complaints.'

'Seeing her again?'

'Wednesday night.'

'Why not before?'

'Don't want to seem too eager. Keep her guessing a bit,'

he said, smiling.

'No. The real reason is that I'm going to be busy this week, and Wednesday's the only night I'll be free. I promised the Works Manager that I'd have a report ready for him by next weekend, and I've still a few odds and ends to tidy up.'

'What kind of report?' asked Tony.

'Well, production has been unreliable for the last six months. We've had some excellent days, but also some very bad ones. There was a meeting to investigate the causes for this, and at the end of it each department had to nominate someone to look at the problems and make a report – discussing it, of course, with other people in the department. Jack here was the lucky one in the lab.'

'What have you found so far?' asked Ray.

'Nothing revolutionary. Our department have felt for some time now that the main reason is the variability of the machine operators. We work three shifts, and it's hard to say this definitely without a detailed analysis. I'm in the process of producing a series of graphs that I hope will throw some light on it.'

'Not a job for a chemist, I would have thought,' said Tony.

'We're trying to vindicate ourselves. We know that at least one other department thinks that the main trouble is the quality of the glass, which is our responsibility. You know, batch mixing, analysis, and all that sort of thing. We've carried out comprehensive analyses and controls, and are convinced that this isn't the case. And so, besides producing the results of these investigations, we are going to try and pinpoint what's at fault.'

'How did you come to be given the job?' said Ray.

'The Chief Chemist thought that as I was young and fairly fresh out of college, the experience would be valuable. It's made a welcome change from the routine stuff.'

'Do you have to read out the report?'

'No. Each department has to circulate copies of its report, so that it can be studied. Then there's another meeting and all the proposals will be discussed. I will have to reply to anything raised concerning our report.'

'What if the graphs don't show anything?' said Ray.

'Well, it's not wasted. It eliminates the operators from suspicion. I'm convinced though that they'll show this to be at least a contributory factor. The early results point that way.'

'Can't you do all this during working hours?' asked Tony.

'I was hoping to be able to, but I've collected such a mass of data that the only way to have it ready in time is to work in the evenings as well. I can do more in two hours at home than in a whole day at work. Although I'm on this project I'm still called upon to do various other things.'

'Pints all round again?' asked Ray.

'Please!' said Ken.

'Pint for me, Ray,' said Tony.

Ray gathered the empty glasses and went to the bar. Most of the people present were playing either cards or dominoes, and on the way Ray stopped at one or two tables to offer advice on how the hand should be played or which domino dropped next. His advice was usually good-humouredly and rudely ignored.

'How did Mary react?' Ken asked Tony.

'I got in first, suggesting having dinner out, so – so far so good. I told her that I spent the night with you, going to your place for supper. She thinks that you're a quiet type and approves. Had I said I'd been with Ray, that would have been a different thing.'

'I'd better be careful what I say.'

'If you would.'

Ray returned with the beer, saying, looking at Tony, 'Your friend won't serve me. She stands at the other end of the bar, pretending she hasn't seen me.'

'I noticed the landlord talking to you,' replied Tony.

'Talking to me. That's a laugh. I said to him, "Lovely day," and in reply he grunted. I then said, "Been a good session for you," and he didn't even grunt. I was determined he'd have to say something, so after he pulled the beer I stood there without offering the money. He was annoyed, but eventually said, "That'll be four and six." I gave him a five pound note. The so-and-so gave me three notes and the rest in silver.'

'He won, then?'

'Afraid so,' replied Ray, sitting down and resting his legs on a stool. They talked about the previous evening's happenings and what the papers had to say about the football and cricket.

'Well, I must be off. Mustn't be late for dinner,' Ken said, rising.'

'Will you be out tonight?' Ray asked.

'Maybe. Depends how far I get. If my mother goes out this afternoon and I get a clear run at it I may manage the last hour. But you won't be available.'

'We'll be in the Imperial later on, so if you're interested come along.'

'Two's company.'

'Oh – Pat's friend will be there. She's coming back on the nine o'clock bus and Pat's promised to meet her in the car.'

'What's the friend like?'

'Pat says she's most attractive, but she's engaged. That's why she goes home at weekends.'

'I'm not saying for certain that I'll be there. So long.'

'Try and make it. Tony and Mary are coming . . . Mary's got the night off.'

'So long,' they both replied.

As he went out he shouted 'Cheerio' to Mary, who was now standing at that end of the bar. She beckoned him across, and asked him what the dance had been like. He replied that it had been much as usual and that he and Tony had come home together. She looked at him a little unbelievingly. He kept his face immobile without giving a hint that he realized that she was fishing. He remarked to her that he hoped she'd enjoy the dinner at the country club. She smiled and said that she was looking forward to it. He said, 'See you again,' and walked towards the door. He glanced at Tony and then back to the bar. Mary was out of sight and he put up his thumb to indicate that all was OK. Tony smiled, looking relieved.

Outside, the atmosphere was heavy and the sky overcast, as though a thunderstorm was imminent. The temperature had dropped and he wished that he'd brought a coat with him. He started running as he felt the first few spots of rain. By the time he reached home it was raining heavily and he was soaked to the skin. His mother was putting the dinner onto the table.

'I'd better get changed first,' he said, and went upstairs.

'Hurry up or the puddings will be spoiled,' she answered, adding, 'I told you to get properly dressed, didn't I?'

He thought of replying that no matter how he was dressed he would still have got wet, decided it wouldn't convince her of anything, and said nothing. He rubbed his hair with a dry towel and changed all his clothes.

Over dinner he read the *New Scientist* and film reviews in the newspaper supplement. His mother was reading a women's weekly journal. There had been a time when reading during meals was strictly taboo, but the conversion was now complete. His father had always been allowed this privilege, but no one else. Ken had complained persistently about the injustice of this and had gradually got his own way. Dinner was always simple, but delicious. He couldn't remember a Sunday dinner which he hadn't relished. On the occasions when he'd been away from home, Sunday lunchtime had been a constant reminder of his mother's superb cooking ability. To start there was a Yorkshire pudding which covered the whole plate. The edges were crisp and curled, serving to contain gravy. To follow was roast mutton or beef, potatoes, two other vegetables and gravy, all cooked to perfection.

After dinner he helped wash up, and then stretched out on the settee in the front room, listening to a repeat of a comedy show which had been broadcast the previous week. He was feeling drowsy, and he very soon nodded off. He awoke about an hour later, another cup of coffee on the table in front of him and his mother telling him to drink it before it went cold. He put two heaped teaspoonfuls of sugar in and sipped it slowly.

His mother asked, 'What time did you get in last night?' indicating that she hadn't believed him.

'I told you.'

'I didn't go to bed till twelve, and then I read for a while.'

'It may have been one. My watch had stopped.'

'It was later than any one o'clock.'

He didn't reply.

'Where did you go?'

'Dancing, as I do every Saturday night,' he replied, mildly irritated.

'The dance finishes at half past eleven.'

'I went to Tony's for a bite to eat.'

'I'll bet you did. Anyway, I hear that he's going about with that barmaid in the pub.'

'Who told you that?'

'Never mind.'

'People want to mind their own business.'

'It's true then?'

'I didn't say that.'

'Are you going out tonight?'

'I'm still working on my report. I want to do at least three hours at it tonight. I may go out later. Will you be going out?'

'I'm going to Alice's for tea, and staying the evening. I'll leave your tea ready before I go. How's the report coming along?'

'So – so. Last week I was thoroughly browned off. Every time I sat down to try and put the pieces together somebody interrupted me with some triviality or other. I felt like tearing it up.'

You want to make a good job of it. The right people will notice it then.'

'What right people?' he asked, indignantly.

'You know what I mean.'

He picked up a magazine, not wishing to say anything further, deciding that he'd wait till after tea before doing any work. During his student days he had often worked throughout Sunday, and now he wondered however he'd managed it. Since graduating, weekends had become an orgy of leisure. He had a cigarette, and then curled up again on the settee. Meanwhile, his mother had changed and was almost ready to go. He asked if she wanted him to take her in the car. As he had some work to do she said 'No,' and set off. Alice was an old friend of the family, whom his mother visited from time to time. She was a very genteel lady, and when she visited them he tended to tease her. She took it in good part, and he liked her for it.

He had a light tea, and forced himself to get out the briefcase containing the figures necessary for the graphs. He still felt lethargic, and had no appetite for it. He made the surface area of the table-top as large as possible, and spread out all the relevant papers. In no time at all he was completely engrossed. He worked quickly and surely. His head seemed to clear and things started to make sense. The graphs were coming out as he'd hoped, producing a feeling of elation. New ideas kept coming to him which he was able to incorporate in the final scheme. Time seemed to stand still, and when he glanced at the clock he was surprised to see that he'd been occupied for three and a half hours. He sat back to survey what he'd done. Now he felt drained, but highly satisfied. He packed the papers away ready for the next morning, and burned the pieces of paper he'd used for rough work. Figures were still flashing about in his brain as he changed into flannels and a sports coat.

8

ENTERING THE IMPERIAL HOTEL, he bumped into an old school friend whom he hadn't seen since his school days. They went into the bar together. Ray, Pat, Tony and Mary were sitting at a table with two other couples whom Ken didn't recognize. There were no other vacant seats. Pat was the first to notice Ken. She smiled and waved. Her hair was shining, her cheeks glowing. He couldn't take his eyes off her. He made a half wave in reply, and moved to the bar. Ray, seeing Pat wave, turned to see who she was waving to. Seeing Ken he looked to see if there was room to fit him in around the table. Ken quickly went across to them and said that he'd met this old school pal and would be happy enough at the bar.

He returned to stand at the bar, his friend having ordered two glasses of beer. They asked each other about what had happened to them since leaving school, and whether they knew what the other lads of the same year were up to now. Revelations flowed furiously. Once this subject was exhausted they started reminiscing. Do you remember such an incident, or that particular master? Ken was enjoying it. The figures and the graphs were pushed out of consciousness and he savoured the nostalgia. He felt amused by the whole episode. Whenever his father had related his past glories, as a footballer or a committee member of the British Legion, Ken had poked fun at him, and given an opportunity would mimic him. Only if he overdid it was his father ever annoyed. At the ripe age of twenty-five, here he was indulging in the same thing. The recollections seemed endless. Although so much occupied, he kept in touch with the goings-on at Ray's table. The conversation appeared strained. Ray, trying as hard as ever, didn't seem to be getting much response. Mary was talking to one of the women he didn't know, and Tony admiring the decorations on the ceiling. Pat looked bored and glanced about the room, occasionally catching Ken's eye. He looked away immediately, not wanting to give the impression that he was taking much interest. He thought that Pat's friend mustn't have returned, because she didn't speak to either of the women and they were obviously friends of Mary.

The stories of old times eventually dried up and he decided to go home. His friend stayed to have another drink. He said 'Goodnight,' and waved goodnight to the others.

His mother was home, and he had a hot drink and a biscuit before going to bed. He asked to be called early in the morning, as he wanted to get to the factory in good time before the others in the department arrived. In bed he went over the day, and felt satisfied. He found his thoughts returning again and again to Pat. He slept soundly.

9

THE NEXT MORNING he got up at six and left home at seven. Normally he didn't start work till eight-thirty, but he wanted an hour on his own. As he passed the time office, the clerk asked him if he knew what time it was. He smiled and replied that he did. He went into the laboratory and changed into his white coat. The day shift was in full swing and he knew which operators would be working. We wanted to talk to a couple of them, whom he was able to confide in, and discuss the findings so far. They had been of assistance to him, and he wanted to let them know how things were turning out. They hadn't been speaking out of turn or telling tales, but giving Ken information that only someone with first-hand knowledge of the job could know about.

Walking through the factory he received surprised looks and the odd remark as to whether he suffered from insomnia. He didn't keep himself aloof from the work-people. He often stopped and asked them about their particular job, even if it had no direct bearing on his department. If he sometimes got stuck with an analysis and felt like a change of scene he would stroll around the factory, chatting to the operators and sorters. One or two of the managers had noticed this and didn't approve, although nothing had actually been said to him. The looks he got as they passed were sufficient to show what they were thinking.

The noise of the machinery jarred his nerves. He was still a little sleepy, and the noise produced a thumping feeling in his head. First he went to see the shift foreman. As he entered the office the foreman looked embarrassed and a bit guilty. He was sitting in front of a small coal fire, drinking from a huge pot of tea and eating a sandwich.

One of the checkers was also there with a mug of tea in his hand. Seeing Ken he muttered something about having to go and see how the packers were managing, and departed leaving the mug, almost full, on the table.

To try and put the foreman at ease, Ken said, 'Relax. I'll join you with a cup if there's one in the pot.'

The foreman fumbled in the cupboard above his desk, and produced a cup without a handle. He was going to put it back.

'It'll do,' said Ken.

He poured the tea, which was thick and dark, and handed it to him.

'Sorry, no milk,' he said.

'That's OK. Perhaps it'll waken me up.'

The foreman sat down again, now more at ease.

'What can I do for you?' he asked.

'First of all I'd better apologize for giving you a fright,' Ken replied, smiling at him. 'I've come early to get the weekend production figures and see some of the operators. I'm still doing the report I told you about, and I may be able to use this weekend's figures.'

The foreman looked among a pile of papers on his desk and then handed a large sheet to Ken, saying, 'I had a quick glance when I came at six, and they don't look too good.'

Ken looked at the sheet and said, 'Number two furnace is still doing well.' Then, as he read further, 'Look at six, that's low. What caused that?'

'Oh, someone told me about that. Let me think. Ah, yes. The temperature was all to cock.'

'Is it alright now?'

'Better, but still on the low side.'

'On the whole it looks a poor weekend. What do you think about it all?'

'Wouldn't like to commit myself. I think what your boss says is part of the trouble. When I first started here, twenty years ago, to become an operator took a three year's apprenticeship, but now we've got some operators who've only been with the firm a year – even less in some cases.'

'It's changed a bit since then, though.'

'Yes, I know that, but you still need a fair amount of skill that can only come with experience,' he replied, lighting a pipe and standing.

He looked out of the window and pointed with the stem of the pipe at one of the furnaces.

'Tek him, for instance. Yon chap there started as a sorter not six months back.'

'What's he like?'

'Well, you can't really tell. He's in my shop one day and somewhere else the next. He tries hard, but whether he's consistent I just don't know.'

'Anyway, we may know something soon.'

'When's the next meeting?'

'Next Friday. Is Bill working this morning?'

'Yes, on number one. Pity they're not all like Bill.'

'Good, is he?'

Ken knew that he was, but wanted to hear the foreman's opinion, because he also knew that Bill hadn't a high opinion of the foreman.

'None better. Started at the same time as me. We were both twenty, just come out of the army. There's nowt you can tell Bill about this job.'

Ken nodded and then said, holding up the sheet, 'All right if I have this for half an hour? I'll return it when I've copied the figures.'

'Sure you can, lad,' he replied. 'So long as it's back here for dinner time, that's all that matters.'

'I may not get down again myself, and if not I'll send one of the young lads,' he said as he opened the door.

'How many of them lads have you got now then?' the foreman asked. 'There are more different faces about t'place than ever,' he continued.

'Only four.'

'What do they do?'

'Help with the apparatus and do simple operations. They go to the tech one day a week.'

'Going to be chemists, are they?'

'That's the idea.'

'We'll have more chemists than owt else,' he replied, laughing.

'Nice people, though,' Ken replied, also laughing.

'Sometimes, sometimes.'

Ken put the cup, which was still half full, down on the table. The foreman followed Ken out and they walked together towards number one furnace. The foreman stopped to talk to one of the sorters. Ken thanked him for his trouble and proceeded. Even though the shift had only been in progress two hours the operators were already covered in grime and grease. Bill was sitting on a broken box, mopping his brow with his shirt sleeve.

'Warm, this morning, Bill?'

He looked up, surprised.

'Hello. Bloody is Ken. Have a seat.'

He stood the other half of the box on its end, and covered it with a flattened carton.

'Thanks,' he said, and sat down.

'What brings you here so early?'

'The report. Thought I'd collect the figures before the rest of 'em get here. Once they arrive everything stops for two hours.'

'What are this weekend's like?'

'Not so good.'

'I hear they were short of men.'

'The foreman didn't mention it.'

'He wouldn't. Probably doesn't even know, too busy supping tea.'

Ken didn't wish to get involved in this, and quickly

100

changed the subject.

'Get to the match on Friday?'

His face brightened, and he said, 'Yes. That young lad on the left wing had a good game, don't you think?'

'Didn't go down. They reckon so though.'

'If they keep that team we should win a few matches.'

Ken noticed that he was almost out of breath when he'd finished speaking.

'Do you feel alright Bill? You look hot and flushed.'

'I'm OK. It gets hot, that's all.'

'Yes, but you shouldn't be out of breath like you are.'

'I'll never get any better,' he replied.

'Why not? Is it asthma?'

'Sort of. The doctor says that I worked in too much heat when I was younger. I used to clean out the furnaces and get them ready again. The heat was terrific.'

They discussed various aspects of an operator's job. Bill had a tendency to criticize all and everything, and Ken tried to keep him to the points he was interested in, carefully steering him off the emotional issues.

The foreman approached.

Bill stood up and put on his protective gloves, whispering, 'Whoever showed this bloke how to grease arses certainly did a good job.'

Ken couldn't contain his laughter.

As the foreman came to them Bill said to him cheerily, 'Now then, my old cock, you look pale this morning. Had your six monthly work-out this weekend?' nudging Ken as he said it.

The foreman hadn't much sense of humour, and Bill knew it and played on it.

'Never mind that. How's bottles coming out this morning?' he replied, unsmiling. The foreman didn't like Ken talking with Bill, and usually interrupted them if he saw them together.

'Round and hot,' Bill answered, winking at Ken.

Disregarding this, the foreman said, 'They're having trouble wi' necks up yonder, so watch 'em will you?'

He walked away without waiting for a reply.

'The only neck I have bother with is his. It's too bloody long. He can't keep his nose out of owt.'

'Don't let it worry you,' said Ken, patting him on the shoulder.

'May see you later.'

'OK. So long, Ken,' he replied.

'Bill had told him all he wanted to know, so he decided against seeing the other operator. There were a few details from the weekend he still required, and he could get them from the Production Notice Board. To reach it he had to pass through the packing department, in which only girls and women were employed. When he first started work he'd hated having to go anywhere near them. He had no protection against the suggestive comments and attention that was directed at him. He usually retreated, blushing and speechless – to their great amusement. Although now hardened to it, he still felt vulnerable.

Pushing the door open, he braced himself. The room was about forty yards in length, and all the girls were sitting at the opposite end to the door that he entered. They were having their mid-shift tea break. They worked shifts and had started at 6.00 a.m. Some of them were knitting, the others having tea, or coffee from flasks. They looked up as they heard the door open. The other door was at the end they were sitting at. One of the girls stood up and made as if to go weak at the knees in a faint.

'Isn't he gorgeous?' said another.

They all tittered. He looked straight ahead and walked towards them, his face expressionless.

'Do you think he's got a big 'un?' he heard one of them say quite deliberately in a loud enough voice so that he heard what was said.

They laughed even more.

102

They all burst into renewed laughter.

He tried to stifle a smile, but wasn't successful. When he was within five yards of them he said, 'Morning girls.'

A few of them replied, 'Morning.'

Passing them, one said, 'Aren't you going to stop and talk to us?'

'I'm in a hurry. I've a lot to do this morning.'

He could feel the blood going to his face and made an effort to control it.

'Well, *have* you?' a voice asked.

There was a complete silence.

Without stopping, he replied, 'Enormous!'

They all burst into renewed laughter.

He closed the door quietly behind him and shook his head from side to side in amusement. He copied the statistics he required and returned to the lab – taking the long way round through the storage yard, not wishing to see the girls again.

Besides himself and the four youths, there were in the department two more assistants and a chief chemist. Two women were also employed to wash the apparatus and to do any other cleaning work. The chief was a quiet introspective man of about fifty. He didn't interfere much, and was always approachable for advice.

When he arrived back, all the others were busy, picking up where they'd left off on Friday evening.

'Thought you weren't coming this morning,' one of them remarked, 'and you're here all the time.'

'Keen, aren't we?' another said.

'You know how it is,' he replied. 'Got to get this in for Friday,' taking up a bundle of sheets from the bench.

He asked one of them if he'd mind completing an analysis for him so that he could continue with the report. He cleared a corner of the bench and scrutinized the new figures to see if he could fit them into the graphs. After half an hour the chief arrived and, before going into his office, came up to him.

'How's it coming along Ken?' he asked.

'Fine, have a look at these,' passing him the graphs.

'Complicated, aren't they?' he said.

'Not really. I'll be attaching an explanation and a summary.'

He explained the relevance of each one. The chief looked impressed and asked if he might have them for a couple of hours to study.

'Of course,' he replied.

On Monday mornings, for an hour before lunch, Ken had to check the work of one of the students. The chief set them some simple problems on Friday evening, which had to be completed for Monday. The lad was extremely shy, and no matter how Ken tried he had difficulty getting more than a couple of words at a time from him. He was intelligent, and presented good neat work. After marking the work and explaining the difficulties that had arisen, he questioned him about the work he did at the 'tech'. Ken soon ran out of interesting things to ask, so gave him the sheet which had to be returned to the foreman, telling him where to go and who to ask for. It was twenty minutes before lunch, and he didn't return till two minutes after the buzzer had blown.

'Get lost?' Ken asked him, smiling.

His face was red and he looked at the floor, rubbing behind his ear with his index finger.

After a few seconds he replied, 'No.'

'Did you see Mr Jones himself?'

'Yes,' he answered, his eyes moving up and down.

'What kept you so long?'

'Well, I asked the way and somebody directed me to the wrong place.'

'Where did you get to?'

'The carton packing department,' he replied, going a deep scarlet.

'Were they rude to you?'

He didn't answer, but took a deep breath and rubbed his hands together.

Ken went up to him and ruffled his hair.

'You'll get used to them. They're like that with all the men, especially if you're new and young.'

The lad smiled, looking a little embarrassed.

'Are they?' he said, seeming relieved.

'You'd better be off for dinner, or you'll be too late.'

'Are you coming to the canteen?'

'No, I'm going into town.'

10

He drove into town and parked in a side-street off the main street. He'd ordered a textbook on statistics at the library, and had received a card to say that it was available.

The library was almost empty, and he quickly obtained the book. He had to fill in a special form, as he wanted to keep it for longer than the usual two weeks. He attempted to say something to the young assistant, but she didn't take much notice. He handed her the completed form and thanked her.

The streets were crowded with lunchtime shoppers. In the bank there was a long queue. The majority of those waiting were business people, paying in their weekend's takings. The cashier had to check three sets of figures and the cash. Also there were only two girls behind the counter. The others were obviously taking lunch. He felt like going up to the counter and saying, 'I only want this cheque cashing, could you oblige?' He knew the girl wouldn't object, but the 'self-made' men would certainly take exception to it. He waited patiently. The man immediately in front of him had a brown case, and he produced from it what seemed an endless series of money bags and paying-in slips. The girl was checking them off as quickly as possible, flicking through the notes and weighing the silver almost simultaneously. He took out a large blue bag and said that was the last. The girl took a deep breath and smiled. When she'd checked it he moved to one side to arrange his bags and slips in the case. Ken handed her a cheque saying that he wouldn't occupy her for long. He noticed that she was moist with perspiration. She passed him the cash, counting it out note by note. He wanted to stay and talk to her for a while, as he normally did, but as she was so busy he just took the notes and said, 'Bye.'

'Cheerio, Mr Appleyard,' she replied, taking as she did so the next customer's books. As he left, the man with the brown case was still there, oblivious of his surroundings, absorbed in the contents of the case.

He had an hour in which to have lunch and return to work. He made his way to a small snack bar where they served a good sandwich and a cup of tea which was drinkable. It was never crowded, and he had been able, on the few occasions he'd been there, to have a table to himself and spread out a newspaper or quietly read a novel or magazine. The people who owned it were foreign, probably Cypriots he thought, and the clientele was mainly middle-aged clerks and shop-assistants. There was no jukebox, and so no teenagers. He ordered a beef sandwich, a scone and a cup of tea, and retired to a corner of the room which was in the shade. As he ate he skimmed through the book to try and find the subjects he required. He found a page that looked promising, and started to read it carefully. After a few minutes he sensed that someone was looking at him.

A woman's voice said, 'Do you mind if I join you?'

He looked up. It was Pat. She was standing in front of the table with a tray in her hands, smiling at him with her eyes. She was simply dressed – in a plaid skirt, white blouse and an olive green cardigan – with a shopping bag slung over her arm. Ken hesitated, then said, 'Hello. Sure. Plenty of room,' moving his used plates out of the way and closing the book.

'Thanks,' she replied, and sat down, removing from the tray a plate containing a solitary éclair and a cup of coffee.

'Is that your lunch?' he asked, looking at the éclair. She laughed, and said, 'Hmm. Must watch my figure.'

He looked her straight in the face, then moved his head to one side, conspicuously looking at her legs, and said,

'Can't see what you've to worry about.'

'That's because I'm careful,' she replied.

'Were you called Fatty at school?'

'Not quite, but I was plumpish.'

'Why do you prefer the slim Pat to the plump Pat?'

'Oh, I'm neurotic about my weight. Being slim means I can wear all the clothes I enjoy wearing.'

There was a short pause, and then he said, 'You looked bored last night.'

'I was,' she replied, and followed with, 'but please don't tell Ray.'

'He could probably tell anyway. Who were the two other couples?'

'Friends of Mary. I think I said two words to them all evening.'

'What were they talking about?'

'From the snatches I caught, it sounded to be a progress report on who was sleeping with whom, or something equally dreary.'

'That's dreary, is it?' he said, raising his eyebrows.

'It is if you don't know the people concerned.'

'Yes, I suppose you're right.'

'Have you known Ray long?' she asked.

'All my life. We went to the same infant, junior and grammar schools.'

'And the same university?'

'No. No. I went to a less fashionable one, where glass technology could be studied. Ray's an Oxford man, you know.'

'I didn't know, but I'm not surprised. He does seem very bright.'

'Yes, a good second class honours in history, he got.'

'You work at the glassworks?'

'Your perception frightens me,' he teased her. 'That's right,' he replied, picking up a glass ashtray off the table. 'I help to ensure that things like these come out nice and pure and clear,' he continued.

'Do you like it?'

'The pay's good.'

'You don't sound thrilled.'

'I'm not.'

'What would you like to do?'

'Dunno. What do you do?'

'Hasn't Ray told you?'

'He did say something about being a high-class prostitute, but I suppose you must do something else in your spare time.'

She didn't appear shocked, and said, 'He said that, did he? Wait till I see him.'

She rested her elbow on the table, and gazed through the window as though in deep contemplation. He didn't really know her at all, and yet they were immediately at ease with one another. He looked at her hand as she gently tapped the table.

'Well, are you going to tell me?' he asked, breaking the silence.

She looked at him, and said, 'I'm sure Ray must have told you.'

'Why all this secrecy?'

'There's no secrecy. I did tell Ray, but it sounds as though he didn't believe me.'

'What did you tell him?'

'That I sold contraceptives.'

Ken smiled at her, looking mildly surprised and trying to appraise whether she was joking or not.

She looked back at him with a calm and serious demeanour.

'Don't you believe me?' she asked.

'I suppose not,' he replied, 'unless you work in a chemist's shop or one of those backstreet herbalist-type places – which I don't think you do.'

'No, I don't.' I'm helping to promote these new oral

110

contraceptives.'

'The pill, in other words?'

'That's it.'

'And this town of ours has been singled out for your particular attention?'

'Oh, no. It happens to be conveniently situated for my area. I cover a territory including South Yorkshire and Sheffield.'

'What are you doing here, today, in that case?'

'Well, this week I'm doing this area. This afternoon I'm talking to a Mothers Union meeting at the parish hall in Hickton.'

'I thought you said you weren't a fairy godmother helping people in need?'

'I didn't think of it like that at the time. And anyway, the majority of the women I help aren't in need. The ones we'd really like to help, we very rarely see. Unfortunately, in one respect, it's only the middle-class, highly-organized mothers who come and enquire, but we're working to change this.'

'However did you get into a job like this?'

'I have a semi-medical background. I'm a qualified hospital biochemist and I saw an advertisement in one of the journals and applied. At the interview I must have made a good impression, and they accepted me for the training course.'

'Is it a government post or one of the drug concerns you work for?

'Private enterprise. The parent company is American. We were the first firm to put such a pill on the market.'

'So you will have bumped off more women with thrombosis than any other firm?'

'You've been reading too many press articles.'

'There must be some connection.'

She picked up his book and said, 'Statistics, which it seems you know something about, refute this.'

111

'Statistics can be made to prove anything you wish.'

'Oh no they can't.'

'How many years has it been on the market now?'

'I'm not certain, but a few.'

'And there are women who have been taking it for years?'

'Yes.'

'And there have been no really bad side-effects?'

'No.'

'So the statistics show.'

'I'll never convince you.'

'Another point to be remembered is that a woman's creative span is perhaps thirty years,' he said, feeling pleased with himself for having thought of this.

'We certainly can't be dogmatic. We will have to wait and see and record all the manifestations that arise. I read an article recently that produced figures which indicated that women taking the pill were less likely to get certain forms of cancer, so there are compensations.'

'That's if they don't die of thrombosis before they get to the age that cancer usually sets in.'

'You're hopeless,' she replied, smiling at him.

'A searcher after the truth,' he answered. Continuing, he asked, 'It's beyond my comprehension how this pill works.'

'Quite simple really,' she replied. When a woman becomes pregnant the body produces a hormone which inhibits the maturation of other egg cells, so that the uterus can prepare for a pregnancy without, as you might say, being interfered with. The pill is a small quantity of a similar progestogen, acting on the ovary in such a way that no eggs enter the reproductive tract and hence conception can't possibly take place. That's it very roughly. It's not *quite* so simple, and there are different types of pill which work in a different way. There's a lot of research being done on suitable dosage levels – we're improving it all the

112

'However did you get into a job like this?'

time. Understand?'

He sat, fascinated, as she reeled this off.

'Amazing,' he replied. 'The thing that strikes me is that it doesn't seem at all natural.'

'Progesterone is a natural product.'

'Pro what?' he asked, looking fogged.

She smiled and said, slowly, pausing after each syllable, 'Progesterone – that is, pro gestation – in favour of pregnancy. Although, to be fair, it is a progesterone-like substance we use.'

'Your insight makes me feel awfully inferior.'

'Oh, there's nothing to it once you understand the principles and master one or two technical terms.'

'I'm really very impressed, because anything that helps women to stop having ten kids must be a good thing.'

'Well, we are moving out of that age at long last, and not before time. I'm really enjoying the work, because apart from seeing women's groups I feel I'm helping to educate the general practitioners, many of whom qualified before the pill was discovered. It's quite a challenge.'

'How do you manage with the Roman Catholic doctors? We've quite a few of them in this town, you know.'

'I know that. I go to see them, and they're very polite and listen to what I've got to say. And some, I do know, are prescribing it – though not for their Roman Catholic patients of course.'

'That's good to hear; the bit about prescribing it, I mean.'

Ken then stood up and picked up his book.

'I must be off. I start work at half past one. I've enjoyed our little chat, and there you are – you've made another convert to your cause. I'll see you again, no doubt. Bye.'

'Bye.'

Driving back to work, Ken had a feeling that he'd be seeing a lot more of Pat. She was easy to get along with, and they seemed to be on the same wavelength. He felt quite envious of Ray, but also felt uneasy for him. Ray liked women and had formed relationships, but they never seemed to last. He knew Ray worried about it, but seemed at a loss to get to the bottom of it. Pat might be the last straw. He'd noticed already that he was very strongly attached to her – and who could blame him? If this one didn't get off the ground Ken knew that Ray would be in for a rough time. Ken was also attracted to Pat, but he resolved that whatever happened he must not undermine Ray in any way whatsoever. He'd got to help him if at all possible. As he drove through the works' gates he crossed his fingers for him – he was going to need all the luck he could get.

11

JACK PEARSON, the chief chemist at the glassworks, was in his early fifties and had spent his whole working life at Tomlinsons Limited. He had not been conscripted, because of his short-sightedness. He'd started, aged fifteen, when the laboratory department consisted of three people only. The works had moved site, so that it could expand, in the early nineteen-forties; and as the works had grown, so had the laboratory. He had studied at the local technical college and had obtained his qualifications in that way.

The previous Chief Chemist had been a woman, Edith Copley, and she'd treated him like the son she'd never had. What she didn't know about making glass wasn't worth knowing. Everything she knew she passed on to Jack Pearson – he was such a diligent eager pupil, with a quiet respectful manner. When she had retired, five years ago, a successor was tailor-made and ready and waiting. The post wasn't advertised. Jack just moved up a place. It suited everybody.

If anything, Jack was too conscientious. Ken knew that he took a lot of work home, and thought that this wasn't a good idea – not on a regular basis at any rate. Miss Copley, apparently, had hardly ever done this, but she was a stronger and more confident personality, with forceful powers of motivation and leadership. She'd been much loved at Tomlinsons, and when she retired they gave her a royal send-off. She hadn't left the district on her retirement; she had too many friends and interests in the area for that to happen, and she still popped in occasionally to see them. When she did, the place took on another dimension. She sparkled, and this was infectious. Any newcomer since she had left was quickly made a friend and became part of the team. Ken had taken to her straight away. He'd known her a little in his labouring days, when a student, but now he'd got to know her really well. She was so proud of this department. In the early days the lab people were treated by the senior management as a bit of a luxury. She had changed all that. 'Them with their heads in the clouds', was how they had once described the lab people, and it was a phrase with which she had mildly rebuked them, when appropriate, over the years that followed. She kept abreast of all the latest developments which could help the company, and the respect had grown and grown. She could still converse knowledgeably about recent innovations, and Ken and some of the younger ones felt a bit shamed at times. She had built a small empire within the company by taking on work that wasn't really their work – she'd done this out of sheer enthusiasm and energy, not for any reasons of self-aggrandizement. This, of course, had created problems when she retired. Ken had often wondered if she had realized that this would be the case and whether that's why she called in – just to help Jack if she could. Jack was always glad to see her, and his load did seem lighter after one of her visits.

Ken was puzzled as to why she'd never married. She was still an attractive lady in her mid-sixties, with her slightly greying hair and straight back. When the subject was broached there was talk of a broken romance in her twenties. What a pity that a woman like this had no children. Ken thought that she would have made a marvellous mother – so intelligent, so full of life. She lived with a sister, a school teacher, who also had never married. And both were contented and well-adjusted people. Whether this had always been the case, Ken didn't know. It was hard to imagine Miss Copley any different, but time can change many things.

Jack Pearson was the only one in the department with his own office; the others shared one. This didn't matter, because most of their time was spent in the lab or in the works. Recently Jack had seemed to spend more time than usual in his office, and although still even-tempered he did seem quieter than normal. He hadn't many interests, his main social outlet being bridge. He was a member of a regular Tuesday night bridge party, and also travelled further afield when in competitions. He had two children, a boy and girl who were both doing well at school, and his wife worked part-time for a local account-ant. It seemed a happy marriage, but lacking excitement.

As Ken made his way back to the lab from the car park he was thinking about these things and his report. Was Jack quieter because of these recent problems at work, or was it something at home? It was hard to make out, because Jack had never got on very well with the Works Manager, who was a dominating sort of personality at the best of times. They had seen a lot more of him in the lab recently, but he was usually closeted with Jack in the office and Jack didn't say much about what was discussed. Ken had noticed that they were in the office when he'd left for his lunch.

'Ah, Ken, I didn't see you in the canteen. Have you been home for lunch today?' Mr Pearson asked as he entered the lab.

'No. As a matter of fact I've been into town. I had to collect a book from the library – about statistics actually – I need to brush up on it to see if it will help with the report,' he replied.

'Yes ... well ... good. You know, I think this after-noon might be a good time to discuss it, if it fits in with your plans,' he said, putting down the flask he was inspect-ing when Ken had arrived.

'There's nothing that can't wait.'

'Shall we go into the office then?'

'Sure. I'll just take my coat off and I'll be with you.'

In the cloakroom Ken speculated that the visit of the Works Manager and this suggestion must be connected.

He hadn't given the impression earlier that he wanted to discuss it today. Ken also thought that he looked and sounded a bit edgy. He wasn't usually like this with him.

It was a small office with just one desk, a coat-stand, and a good stock of books on the walls. Mr Pearson's desk was always tidy – meticulously so. Ken's report was on the desk in front of him.

'Come in, sit down Ken,' said Mr Pearson.

'Thank you Mr Pearson,' said Ken, pulling his chair closer to the table, so that if necessary he could see the report.

'I've spent most of the morning reading this,' he said, picking it up and flicking through the pages.

'It's not quite finished, you know.'

'Yes. I realize that . . . I realize that. I hope you don't mind, but Albert Thompson called in just before lunch and I put him in the picture. I hope you don't mind.'

'I do actually, Mr Pearson,' replied Ken, without trying to hide the fact that he was annoyed.

'Why Ken?' said Mr Pearson, a little uneasily, taking off his glasses.

'Well, like I've just said, it's not yet finished . . . there's that for a start.'

'Well, I thought there would be no harm . . . '

'We all know what Mr Thompson's like,' blurted out Ken. He wished he hadn't said this, but out it had come.

'Like what, Ken?' asked Mr Pearson.

'You know as well as I do,' said Ken.

'Give me your version Ken, please.'

'Let me give you the other reasons first why I think he shouldn't have seen it just yet,' Ken said, stalling for time.

Mr Pearson put his glasses back on and took them off again almost immediately, and Ken noticed a slight tremor as he held them just above the report. Mr Pearson didn't like this kind of thing, but that wasn't going to stop Ken saying his piece. He could have backed down and let it

'I've spent most of the morning reading this,' he said.

pass, but he wasn't going to do so just to appease him.

'You see, I haven't drawn it all together yet, and it would be so easy to get the wrong conclusions if you looked at the results superficially.'

'Point taken, Ken.'

'Let me ask you something, Mr Pearson. You said this morning the graphs looked complicated, didn't you?'

'I did.'

'Did you find them self-explanatory?'

'To be honest, no I didn't.'

'Well, that's the point I'm making.'

'Ken, look, I'm sorry. I honestly didn't think you'd mind.'

'I probably wouldn't have if it had been anybody other than Mr Thompson.' It was out, again.

'What's so wrong with Albert, Ken?' he said, resignedly.

'You know as well as me.'

'For God's sake Ken, tell me,' he said, very irritated.

'OK, if you insist. We all know he hasn't a lot of time for us in the lab, and he wastes no opportunity to have a go at us. It's obvious to everybody. Our results will be all round the factory by now, and the other departments will make mincemeat of us on Friday.'

'I think you're exaggerating a bit.'

'Perhaps.'

'What can I do Ken?'

'Stand up for us more, that's what.'

'Ken, Ken, calm down.'

'I'm calm enough Mr Pearson,' said Ken coolly.

'It's not my style, Ken.'

'I know that, Mr Pearson. Look, I'm sorry. I shouldn't have said what I've just said. I'm sorry.'

'No. If that's how you feel you are quite right to express it. I know Albert's not an easy man, but he's got a lot of responsibility and we've to take that into account.'

121

'I've no time for him. It strikes me he's a good crawler. Everybody says so.'

'Explain yourself.'

'Everybody says he only got the Works Manager's job because he's related to one of the directors and goes to the right chapel.'

'I think this conversation has gone quite far enough, Ken.'

Ken then remembered that Mr Pearson went to the same chapel.

'Look, Mr Pearson, that bit about the chapel. I didn't mean anything about you, you know. You got your job on merit, everybody acknowledges that.'

Mr Pearson dropped the report onto the desk and gave out a big sigh. They were both gathering their thoughts. Ken's eyes looked at the front cover of the *Glass Technology* weekly, the only other item, apart from a telephone, on the desk. He knew that Mr Pearson would have already read and digested his copy by now, and it was only issued on a Saturday. Ken had his copy delivered at home, and he normally managed to read it by Wednesday or Thursday. He thought that perhaps something he'd read in the journal, combined with his report, had prompted Mr Pearson to show Mr Thompson the report. At length Ken broke the silence.

'Have you read this week's journal, Mr Pearson?'

'I have, Ken.'

'Anything of interest?'

'Yes. I think that's why Albert came to see me. The competition's getting fiercer by the day, as you know. Rockville have announced big new investments in that latest American technology.'

'We can compete with them, even so. The investments we've made in the last five years have made sure of that,' said Ken.

'We can if we can improve the efficiency, not otherwise,

122

I'm afraid,' said Mr Pearson, who had now regained his composure and was visibly more relaxed.

'What did Mr Thompson say?' asked Ken.

'Well, he'd read about Rockville and he wanted to discuss our productivity. There's the monthly directors' meeting on Wednesday, and they're sure to grill him about the figures, especially with this latest news. He felt he must try and get something positive to show them.'

'What did you both conclude from my report, as it stands?'

'Not much, Ken. As you said, without the concluding summary to explain a lot of things, there isn't much to go on. I must say, though, I'm very impressed by the amount of work you've put in on this. I am very grateful.'

'Thank you. I've enjoyed doing it, really. It didn't seem like work once I got into it. I just hope some good can come out of it.'

'I'm sure it will.'

'Would you like me to explain some of the graphs etc? It could save a lot of time later.'

'That's a good idea.'

The next hour was spent going through the report. Ken and Mr Pearson had always had a good working relationship and, as Ken explained things, Mr Pearson quickly grasped the thrust of it all.

'I think we've earned a cup of coffee, Ken. We'll have it here today if that's alright with you?'

'Sure it is.'

Mr Pearson picked up the telephone and asked the canteen to send two coffees across for them. The canteen was only just across the yard, and this presented no problems.

'Do you mind if I smoke, Ken?'

'No. Go ahead.'

He took a pipe from a shelf behind him, carefully filled it with Digger Flake, his favourite tobacco, and lit up.

123

'Do you still smoke, Ken?'

'A little – my mother nags me a lot, so I've cut down.'

'You can have one now if you wish.'

'I think I will, if you don't mind.'

Mr Pearson offered him a cigarette from the box in a drawer, which he kept for any visitors who smoked cigarettes.

Two large mugs of coffee arrived, and Ken realized it had been a long time since they had talked about much other than work.

'How's the cricket season gone?' asked Mr Pearson.

'We've done exceptionally well. We're in the semi-final play-off for the league a week on Saturday. Personally I've struggled a bit. As you know, I normally open the batting, but I'm down to number four at the moment to try and regain a bit of form. In fact I think that only my fielding has kept me in the first team.'

'It's a good relaxation for you lad.'

'I love it.'

'Yorkshire have had another miserable season, haven't they? I've still got my member's ticket, but I don't seem to get to see them much these days. You know more about cricket than I do Ken. What's the problem there do you think? You get so many conflicting stories in the papers.'

'Too much arguing, I think. They don't seem to be happy unless they're rowing about something. It's a big committee, with a lot of conflicting interests. They don't seem to be able to pull all in the same direction. The players are good enough, I think, but the atmosphere seems all wrong. Take a small club like ours. If we're at loggerheads, we don't get the results. I think it's just the same with Yorkshire. It's probably caused by the clash of cultures, you know, Mr Pearson.'

'Whatever do you mean by that, Ken?' asked Mr Pearson, looking somewhat puzzled.

'Well, I hadn't thought of it this way until I travelled the

124

county playing cricket for Barnfield. But then it slowly dawned. As you know, Yorkshire is split up into three parts, Ridings. But when this was done a mistake was made. It should have been four. There should have been a South Riding as well as a West Riding – which we're in – a North Riding and an East Riding.'

'Why, Ken?'

'The cultures are so different, you see, conditioned by the environment. Take us in Barnfield and Sheffield – we're not as dour as what I call the real West Riding types around Bradford and Leeds. I'm not criticizing them mind. They're much nearer the Pennines than we are. I know we've got more pits, but our environment is much softer, gentler, and the people generally softer and gentler and more humorous. Round here you even get the men calling other men love. Take Johnny Wardle. I think he's a good example of what I mean.'

'But he could be a bit dour and his own worst enemy at times.'

'I agree. I think all us Yorkshiremen share those traits to lesser and greater degrees. The East Riding, with its agriculture, seems more refined – and the North Riding generally similar and softer, like us. And the committee, you see, is drawn from all these parts – they're such different temperaments. They all push their favourite sons as well, which doesn't help.'

'I think what you said about having four ridings, Ken, may not be the answer – perhaps none would be a better answer. Get rid of the divisions.'

'I'll go along with that, though I can't see it happening,' said Ken, laughing.

'But they've always been like that, and they used to win everything.'

'Ah, but that was when the other counties were weak, and luxuries like those we've just been talking about didn't make much difference. Now I think this discontent makes all the difference.'

'I hadn't thought about it like that, you know.'

'Are you still playing bridge?' asked Ken.

'I am. At times I think it's the only thing that keeps me on an even keel, especially at times like these. My wife as well, of course, she's very supportive. I don't know how she fits everything in and stays so cheerful. You see the children, teenagers now, take a lot more handling, but she copes wonderfully well. You've all that to come Ken. Are you courting?' he asked, smiling.

'Nothing serious. I'm taking my time. I'm too well looked after at home you know,' he said, laughing.

'How is your mother?'

'Fine thanks. She's just had a good holiday and looks really well.'

'Give her my regards. I haven't bumped into her for a while now.'

'Thanks. I'll do that. She's always asking about you.'

'Is she? That's nice to know. I'm glad somebody thinks about me,' he said, laughing and then draining his mug.

'Can I have the report back now, to finish off?'

'Yes, here we are,' he said, passing it across the desk.

'How many copies shall I get done ready for Friday?'

'I think about ten will be sufficient, at this stage.'

'The arrangements for Friday are still the same are they? Ten o'clock Friday morning in the board room, with the Managing Director in the chair?'

Mr Pearson took a deep suck at his pipe and coloured slightly. Ken noticed this, surprised.

'Well, it was really about that that I wanted to speak to you this afternoon, Ken. The arrangements have been altered slightly. From our earlier conversation I now know that you're not going to like what I have to say. The Managing Director is in Germany on Company business, so Albert's in the chair.'

He paused, to gauge Ken's reaction.

126

'That's alright. He'll have to be fair and give us all a hearing,' said Ken.

Mr Pearson took another deep suck.

'He's decided, also, that only departmental heads can attend this meeting. He thinks that if there are too many there we'll just go around in circles.'

Ken had been assured that he would be able to present the report and be present for questions and discussions on any points raised. He'd briefed Mr Pearson well, and felt that Mr Pearson knew exactly the points he was making. What he didn't have confidence in was Mr Pearson's ability to probe and question, in depth, the reports of other departments. He'd be too nice.

'I don't like it, but if that's what he's decided I'll have to go along with it. He's the boss,' said Ken.

'I'm sorry. I did try to persuade him otherwise.'

'OK. We'll just have to see how it goes, won't we? I'll let you have the completed thing on Wednesday afternoon. We'll have time, then, to iron out any small items before Friday.

And with that he got up to leave the office.

As he opened the office door Mr Pearson said, 'There is just one other thing, Ken. You know what you said about Albert and the chapel?'

'Yes.'

'Well let me just say this. Don't believe everything you hear on the shop floor. I know that you know a lot of the men from your student days, and I think it's a good thing.'

He paused.

'You said that as though some people don't think it's a good thing, Mr Pearson,' replied Ken.

'I didn't say that.'

'No. But that's how it sounded.'

'Well, some senior management don't like – how can I phrase it ... your ... fraternising shall we say – like you do.'

'Who, for instance?'

'I'm not going into names.'

'My God, what sort of a place is this? You see, Mr Pearson, and I think you'll agree, my report vindicates this department.'

'I agree, and I'm delighted it does.'

'Yes, but what you don't know, because it's not in here,' he said, waving the report, 'is that I realized that this was probably the case quite early on and so widened the scope of my enquiries.'

'Did you now? You didn't tell me.'

'I know I should have, but I felt you wouldn't like me to do that, so I kept it quiet. But anyway, I've told you now.'

'And might I ask what were these other enquiries?' he asked, a little sarcastically.

'To put it bluntly, man-management.'

'Man-management?' he said, astonished. 'That's not our department at all. You're getting into deep water now, Ken.'

'Perhaps I am, but I think I've turned up some very interesting material. But as it's outside the scope of the report you'll not want to know about it, will you?' he said, returning the sarcasm.

'I certainly do. Remember I am still head of this department, although there are times when I start to wonder. I haven't time today, but I'd be obliged if you could tell me about these other enquiries when I see you on Wednesday.'

'It'll be a pleasure. Cheerio.'

'Cheerio,' replied Mr Pearson, and he sank back in his chair. He'd seen a side of Ken he didn't know existed. He'd always thought him much like himself, really. Quietly conscientious and easy with people. More gregarious than himself, certainly, with his sporting outlets, but essentially very similar. He was having to re-assess. He was very curious to know more, but felt he couldn't take it

128

just at the moment. He needed to let it sink in and take a step back. He'd felt he was beginning to lose control of the situation, and he couldn't afford to let that happen. 'Man-management', he muttered to himself as he picked up the journal and flicked through the pages, shaking his head. He felt much the same as Ken did about Albert Thompson, but couldn't say this to Ken. The only thing he had in common with Albert was their attendance at the same chapel in Barnfield. But he'd gone there as a boy, and he seemed to think that this was the case with Albert, too, although he couldn't be certain because it was a very big chapel and had been so much better attended when he was a child than now. You couldn't remember everybody. As for him being related to the Sales Director, this was definitely the case; but whether it had any bearing on his appointment he didn't know. He'd heard it said, of course, times many, but he'd taken it with a pinch of salt. If people saw something like that they often put two and two together and made five. To be fair, he thought, Albert did a good job. Bluff and gruff, but he got the job done. He wouldn't fancy doing a job like that himself – a sort of pig-in-the-middle between directors and the departmental heads – no thanks! OK, he was well rewarded for it, but as far as Jack was concerned he earned every penny, did Albert. 'I'll have to talk to Ken about him,' he thought, 'because Ken's probably got hold of the wrong end of the stick, and after all he's only been here three years and is still very inexperienced. The impetuosity of youth; I'll put him straight. We'll have a good talk about it on Wednesday.'

The others in the lab had obviously sensed the atmosphere. You couldn't exactly hear what was said in the office when in the lab, but you could get the general drift. Nobody said anything when Ken re-entered. One or two looked up, then quickly looked down again, but the rest carried on with their work. Ken felt like a breath of fresh

129

air, so he went straight out and down the yard which led into the factory. 'I'll go and fraternize,' he muttered to himself, wryly, but then smiling.

* * *

When he arrived home for tea his mother was still ironing, although the table was set ready – the only other thing to be done being the actual mashing of the tea itself.

'Still at it?' said Ken as he entered the living room.

'I've had a lot today, but I'm almost finished now.'

'You should have left some of the ironing for another day.'

'Oh, I like it done with, but I think I will leave the rest until tomorrow, because I'm going out this evening.'

'Where to?'

'It's the first class of the term at night school at Bradstone.'

'What are you doing this year?'

'Decorative stitchery.'

'Sewing, you mean.'

'No. Decorative stitchery,' she replied, a little irritated.

'Is Alice going with you?'

'Yes. In fact she went to that class last year and really enjoyed it. She made some lovely things.'

'What time does it start?'

'Seven o'clock, so I haven't a lot of time – so come on, get your tea so that I can get the table cleared and the pots washed before I go.'

'Does Mrs Pearson still go to the night classes?'

'No. Since she started that part-time job she hasn't really got the time, but I still see her at the whist drives on Thursday nights. She can still manage to fit that in, I'm pleased to say.'

'You'd better not mention my name to her after today.'

'Why ever not? What have you been doing today? I

130

shouldn't tell you this, but from little bits she says I know Jack thinks a lot about you. Surely you haven't been upsetting a nice man like Jack?'

'Well, I think a lot about Jack.'

He could see his mother was looking perturbed. She was flushed.

'Calm down,' he said. 'We've been discussing the report and at one point it did get a bit heated, but no shouting and bawling. We had a cup of coffee and a pleasant chat about his bridge and my cricket and are still on good terms.'

She looked relieved.

'And can I ask why it got heated?'

'He'd shown the report to Albert Thompson this morning. I thought he shouldn't have, and said so. You see it's not finished. I'm staying in tonight and tomorrow night to get it finished – the first meeting is on Friday morning. Also, he tells me that only departmental heads can attend the meeting.'

His mother, by now, was looking more perturbed than before.

'I don't think Mrs Pearson cares much for that Albert Thompson. Anyway, so long as you and Jack are OK, that's the main thing.'

With that she quickly cleared the table, washed up and went to catch a bus to Bradstone, declining Ken's offer of a lift.

12

On wednesday afternoon Mr Pearson called Ken into his office.

'I haven't a lot of time today, Ken, and we went through things pretty thoroughly on Monday, so let's get straight down to the nitty gritty. Have you managed to complete it and tie up all the loose ends?'

As he said this, Ken was still taking his seat and then opening his briefcase. He was surprised by this approach, as Mr Pearson normally took a while to get to the point. He was pleased, though, because he too didn't feel like another long session.

'I have, and I've got the copies done as well.'

He passed the reports across the desk, and then did a quick resume of the summary.

'As we thought, Ken, we've nothing to worry about. Thanks a lot.'

Ken got up to leave.

'Hang on Ken. As that didn't take long, perhaps we could just clear up that other point?'

'Sure,' said Ken, sitting back down.

'Those other investigations you mentioned on Monday – there's nothing about them in here, I notice,' he said, tapping the reports.

'No, there isn't. After what you said on Monday I thought I'd better leave them out.'

'Quite right, but I'd like to know about them just the same – but first of all let me ask you a question. How many people work at Tomlinsons?'

Ken studied for a while, then replied, 'I suppose about six hundred.'

'That's about it, yes. And do you know why I reacted like that on Monday?'

'No, Mr Pearson. I don't if I'm honest.'

'Well, I'll tell you. I've worked here now for almost thirty-five years, and when you mentioned "man-management" my heart sank.'

'Why?'

'You see, I thought we only had six hundred experts on man-management in this factory, and when you said that I thought, "Oh no, not another. That makes six hundred and one." '

'Oh,' said Ken, surprised – and a little taken aback.

'But go on, be brief, tell me your views on this contentious subject.'

'It might save time if you read these.'

Ken gave him two sheets from his briefcase, with facts and figures about his findings. Mr Pearson quickly scanned through them.

'I thought as much,' he said, after reading them.

'What do you mean by that?'

'You probably don't realize it Ken, but these are a direct criticism of Albert and his department.'

'Some of them, possibly, I thought, but not in the main.'

'Take my word for it, they are.'

'OK. I'll accept what you say, but please explain.'

'Well, as you know, the whole object of this exercise is to look at our productivity or rather lack of it. We're not producing enough of the goods at the right time, and orders are being lost. I know the plastics have taken some of the market, but that's only part of the story. Like you said on Monday, it's not for lack of investment. I agree with you on that one. Let me explain about Albert. This business of how he got the job etc. – let's forget about that, because it's not going to help the present situation, is it? Agreed?'

'Agreed. On reflection I think I was a bit hasty on Monday.'

'Right, then. What you don't know about Albert is that

his department is involved in much more than you realize. You can't be expected to know this. It's something that's just evolved over the years. That's why I know your findings point straight at Albert. There isn't time to go into details today, but it is definitely the case. These things have all been looked at before, you can take my word on that.'

'With what results, though?'

'Not many, I must admit. He's a difficult man to cross.'

'Who's crossed him in the past?'

'No names. Let's just say they didn't get very far.'

'Do you intend bringing any of this up on Friday morning?'

'No way, Ken.'

'I see. I suppose I can't complain, because I shouldn't have delved into it, should I?'

'No, you shouldn't, but I think none the less of you for that. Live and learn, eh?'

'I reckon so Mr Pearson. Could I just say something about Mr Thompson that, for obvious reasons, isn't on the sheets?'

'Certainly. We live in a democracy, Ken. Go ahead.'

'A little while ago you asked me a question. Could I now ask you a question, or rather questions?'

'Fire away.'

'How many times do you think Mr Thompson has ever spoken to me?'

'I don't know.'

'None. If I get a nod if we happen to pass in the factory, I've had a good day.'

'He's a busy chap.'

'Secondly, take as an example this new bonus scheme for the shift workers. Why has it made no noticeable difference to productivity?'

'It's true – it hasn't – so go on, tell me why you think that is.'

134

'The consultation before it was introduced was almost nil. Take it or leave it. The men don't like it – it's as simple as that. The morale is also very low. All this talk of cutbacks and redundancies doesn't help – especially when the first they know about it is from the local paper. OK, they may seem small things, but I'm not too sure.'

'You could have a point, but it's just not our department, is it?'

'We'll have to agree to differ on that one,' said Ken, getting up.

'Right, Ken, thanks again. Look, you concentrate on the main thing. We're doing our job well enough, that's our concern.'

'By the way, I was right about the other departments knowing some of our results. I've heard whispers in the canteen.'

'That can't alter the results, so where's the harm?'

Ken could see no point in prolonging the conversation, and left.

13

THAT EVENING, as he was getting ready to go out, his mother asked how his meeting with Mr Pearson had gone.

'Totally disillusioned with him,' was Ken's reply.

His mother was stunned.

'Why?' she asked, eventually.

He explained what had transpired.

'I think Jack's right. You're getting more like your dad, when he was younger, every day.'

'I'm glad you've brought that up, because there's something I want to ask you about. At Dad's funeral I was talking to Percy Hooper, and he said something about his being victimized at Millthorpe and that's how we came to live at North Dene. What was that all about? It was the first I knew about it.'

'Percy had no business telling you about that.'

'Don't blame Percy – he just assumed I knew all about it and it came out in the course of the conversation. It was true then?'

'Yes, but that wasn't the only reason for leaving Millthorpe.'

'Do you think we could talk about it sometime?'

'I'm not sure about that. What's the good in digging up the past?'

'I thought of going to see Percy when you were away, but I thought I'd ask you first.'

'Percy's not well, you'd better not go pestering him.'

'All right, all right, but I'm not just going to forget about it.'

'Are you taking out a dame tonight?' she asked.

'No. I'm going out with a very pleasant young lady, as a matter of fact. To save you asking, we are probably going to the pictures, and I won't be late. Cheerio.'

'Percy had no business telling you about that.'

14

'GOOD MORNING, KENNETH,' said Elsie Copley. 'Is Jack in?'

'No, as a matter of fact it's the first meeting about the reports this morning,' replied Ken. Miss Copley looked surprised.

'In that case, what are you doing here?'

'Oh, Mr Thompson's chairing it and he only wants the top men there. I've put Mr Pearson fully in the picture, so I think things will be all right.'

'You don't sound too sure though, if you ask me,' she said, smiling, and looking at him for clues.

'I'll be honest, I'm not.'

'Why Kenneth?'

'Well, I turned up some stuff that I thought might help, but Mr Pearson has no intention of using it. I can see his point, but I couldn't see the harm it could do. I'll show you.'

He got the two sheets and passed them to her.

'I shouldn't look at them, really.'

'Go on. See what you think.'

'I'll just have a peep then, but don't tell Jack, will you?'

'No. Scouts honour and cross my heart.'

Ken watched her face as she read. It remained expressionless throughout.

On completion she said, 'Yes, I can see why Jack won't use this material, but it's not for me to take sides, you know.'

'I don't want you to. I understand.'

'I had a feeling this might happen one day. You haven't fallen out over it, have you?'

'No, but I've seen Mr Pearson in a new light.'

'It's just not in his nature to get involved in this sort of

138

'Kenneth, you can't ask me a question like that.'

thing. Try to see that.'

'Oh, I do. I know what you mean. Would you have used this material?' he asked.

She burst out laughing.

'Kenneth, you can't ask me a question like that.'

'No. Totally unfair. I'm sorry ... but I bet you would have.'

'Let's just say "perhaps", and leave it at that.'

'I've been wanting to ask you for a while now about how you ever got into the glass industry in the first place.'

Miss Copley proceeded to explain that chemistry had been her best subject at school, that her parents couldn't afford for her to go to college, and that a laboratory assistant was required just as she left school. A natural progression. The Chief before her had been killed at Ypres. She took her chance when it came, and never looked back.

* * *

Ken rented a garage at the top of their street, and as he walked home after work many children were out playing. As he watched them he wondered if they were having a childhood similar to his own. It was hard to speculate what would have happened if his mother and father had never moved to North Dene, but what he was thinking now was how lucky he had been to be planted in this environment, just when he was. 'Victimization' had its good side, he thought.

Over his tea his mother eventually broke the silence.

'Are you going to tell me what happened at work today?'

'There's not much to tell, really. It's been a quiet sort of day.'

'Weren't they having the first meeting this morning?'

'Yes, but Jack didn't say much about it and I didn't feel like asking him. They just went through the preliminaries,

I think. Miss Copley called in this morning.'

His mother's face brightened, as it usually did at the mention of her name. She didn't know her, but liked what she'd heard about her.

'And does Miss Copley know about it all?'

'We did discuss it, yes.'

'And what did she think?'

'Hard to tell. You can't expect her to take sides, but I think she might have pursued it differently from Jack.'

'What makes you think that?'

'Oh. Just the way she reacted, that's all. I may be completely wrong.'

'I think she would have agreed with Jack.'

'I don't see how you can say that when you don't even know her.'

'Just a woman's intuition, that's all.'

'If Dad had been alive he would have been on my side – that I do know.'

'I'm not too sure, but what makes you say that?

'Well, it was one of his hobby horses, wasn't it?'

'How do you mean?'

'Well, he always told me to try and be broad-minded, and I think Jack is being a bit narrow-minded. It hasn't been a wasted exercise though.'

'Why?'

'Well, I've learned a lot from it ... and the main thing I've realized is that I haven't a future at Tomlinsons.'

His mother looked aghast.

'And what do you mean by that, pray?' she spat out.

'Exactly what I said.'

'You're thinking of leaving?'

'Yes.'

'To do what?'

'Dunno, but I've got one or two ideas.'

'Kenneth, you can't be serious. Just you think about it and what you'd be throwing away. Look, this will soon

141

blow over. I know you're upset with Jack at the moment, bit in a week or two it'll all be forgotten.'

'No it won't, that's for sure.'

'What ideas have you got?'

'Teaching, for one.'

'Teaching? You're not qualified as a teacher, so whatever are you talking about?'

'I am qualified. I've a science degree, and that qualifies me. And Ray's headmaster says there's a shortage of maths and science teachers in Barnfield.'

'You wouldn't have the patience for a job like that – and anyway, think of the pay. You wouldn't earn what you do now.'

'I'll ignore the first part of what you said, and the second doesn't bother me.'

'You'd have to sell your car.'

'I doubt that very much. Dad would have approved.'

'Why?' asked his mother, exasperated.

'Well, his first two laws of life would be satisfied – education and experience – that's why.'

'You're not satisfying his third law, though, are you?'

'Which was what?'

'Self discipline, that's what. He wouldn't have approved of all the beer drinking you and your mates indulge in.'

'I reckon he did his share.'

'You never saw him the worse for drink.'

'No, but I think you did.'

'Why?' she asked, looking startled.

'Well, I've been thinking about that one. I know he liked his odd glass of beer towards the end of his life, but I remember that teetotal phase. It caused one or two upsets if I remember rightly, because you thought it ridiculous.'

'I did, and it was!'

'But why should a coal miner be teetotal? I know he drank beer as a young man, so whyever should he become a teetotaller? I can only assume that he must have had some bad experiences with alcohol for this to happen.'

'Who told you that? Percy Hooper was it?'

'No, it wasn't. You've just told me now.'

She picked up the poker from the hearth and prodded the fire. Ken could see that she was ruffled.

'You can't keep quiet about these things for ever you know,' said Ken, when she had settled back in her chair and had regained her composure, though she was still biting her lips.

'I'm saying no more tonight. Are you going out drinking like you usually do on Friday nights?'

'No. We've got the cricket semi-final tomorrow, at Doncaster, so I'm having a bath and an early night.'

'Good,' she said.

'You can come with us if you wish. There will be room on the bus. You haven't seen many matches this season, so why don't you?'

'I think I will if it's a nice day.'

'The forecast's good. You'll enjoy it.'

'Are many going?'

'Oh, yes. All the regulars and a few more besides.'

'I will then. I like cricket, and they're lovely company, the other women. Good idea.'

15

As THE BUS left Barnfield for Doncaster all the omens
were good; the previous night's weather forecast was for a
fine sunny day; Barnfield's opening fast bowler had been
declared fit after a pulled calf muscle; and all the players
had arrived at the ground on time – a most unusual occurrence for some of them. The match had created a lot of
interest in the Barnfield district because this was the first
time for many years that they had managed to get so far in
the competition. They were the underdogs but even so
were quietly confident. Earlier in the season they had lost
to Doncaster but the game had been a close one. Barnfield's success this season was mainly due to their bowlers,
who had been backed up by keen fielding and catching.
The batting had been brittle but, as the bowlers had kept
the opposition's total modest, they had scraped through
some games they would have usually lost. A new skipper
for the season had also made a big difference. He had
played for Barnfield for a long time but had always been
reluctant to assume the captain's role. He had been pre-
vailed upon to have a go at the job by the committee and
was repaying their confidence in him. He had taken on the
position with one main condition – that the players practice and work at their game throughout the whole of the
season and not just for the first month or so as had been
the custom in the past. Some players had balked at this,
but he insisted and even dropped one or two of the better
players for disciplinary reasons. In fact one had left the
club altogether because of this approach. This particular
player had always wanted to be a law unto himself, and
previous captains had allowed him plenty of leeway because of his undoubted ability as a player. The new captain would have none of this and the crunch came in mid

season. They missed him, but it was hard to tell whether it was for the better or worse. The other players were evenly divided in their opinions about this. Some thought he was a great loss, whilst others were glad to see the back of him.

Leaving Barnfield the sun was shining and the bus was full of jokey animated conversations. Approaching Doncaster the atmosphere became quieter as the players anticipated the match ahead. Tension was beginning to creep in. They were a young side, not used to semi-finals. Outside, the sky darkened and the heavens opened. Arriving at the ground they were dismayed to find it under water. A freak cloudburst in the Doncaster area ruled out play for the day. The umpires quickly decided the situation was hopeless. The soccer season had just started so the players asked the driver to get them back to Barnfield as quickly as possible so that they could go and watch the match versus Middlesbrough in the Second Division. This he did readily. Dashing through the turnstiles they asked of the first man they saw, the score.

'Game's over lads,' was the reply.

'How do you mean, they've only been playing twenty minutes?'

'That bloody Clough's scored three already. I'd ask for your money back if I were you.'

'What were they like?'

'Beauties, I've got to admit. Two with his head and a shot from twenty yards.'

For the second time in an hour they were dismayed. Dismayed this time at the score, but also at missing seeing the three goals, because Clough had been one of the magnets that had pulled them back to Barnfield so quickly. The game was effectively over. Barnfield managed to pull a goal back, but that was all.

'The story of my life,' one of them muttered as they trudged away at the end of the game.

The semi-final was played on two evenings the following week, but the atmosphere had gone and Barnfield lost convincingly by six wickets. They had, though, enjoyed the experience of such a big game and felt it would hold them in good stead for the future.

PART TWO
NORTH DENE

16

NORTH DENE was a small estate, erected by a private builder in the mid nineteen-thirties, and the houses rented out. He apparently had chosen the tenants very carefully – no doubt for two good reasons. He wanted the houses well looked after, and the rent paid on time. Most of the tenants were employed in working-class occupations, people such as coal-miners, railwaymen, building workers, plumbers, electricians, glassworks men and the like. As mining was, by far, the biggest industry in the area, the majority of the men were colliers. There were one or two self-employed businessmen and odd ones who managed shops for the local Co-operative Society. These people were the only ones to own cars at that time.

The houses, which were in blocks of four, had two rooms downstairs, three bedrooms and a bathroom, with lavatory upstairs and hot and cold running water. Ken's family lived in a middle one of a block, and to get to the back of the house there was an alley-way or ginnel into which was built the coal-place. Loads of coal were tipped at the front gate and had to be barrowed or bucketed into it. The alley-way, which was about ten feet high, was shared by the people living in the other middle house.

The bathrooms were situated above the alley, and noises from one could be heard in the other. The alley had provided a perfect sheltered outdoor playing area for children in rainy weather. It had taught Ken to straight drive at cricket, because that was the only way runs could be scored when playing cricket in the alley.

There were gardens to the back and front, and a three foot high wall ran down the length of the street. The wall had been useful to Ken for his soccer practice. His father, noticing that Ken was right-footed, told him to practise with his left foot as this would help him when playing football. He spent hours, on his own, kicking the ball against the wall. This certainly paid dividends, because at junior school the football team needed a left full back. The players for the other positions were just about automatic choices. The teacher asked if any of the remaining boys could kick with the left foot. Several said they could. A trial was held, and Ken was fortunate enough to be selected.

He enjoyed the games-playing for the school team. For one thing, they had a moderately successful season. And, in addition, if you were in the team the children in this school regarded you as a bit of a hero. Ken had been surprised when a younger boy had approached him one day in the playground and had asked him for his autograph.

The back gardens were partitioned right up to the houses by a four foot high wooden fence, so that people living in these houses had a good deal of privacy. The front gardens were smaller, and separated by home-made fencing, privet hedges and the occasional quick-thorn hedge. The houses on the other side of the street were constructed in a similar fashion. The whole development only consisted of two streets and a crescent, which formed a semi-circle and led to the main road. The street's surface was of concrete sections, with grates at the centre every thirty yards or so. These made ideal wickets when playing cricket in the street in fine weather.

You could play all the cricket shots in the street, but you had to be careful to keep the ball down low to avoid breaking windows – again good practice. But, of course, accidents did occur. Sometimes, though, the boys were

But, of course, accidents did occur.

lucky. Ray, a bit of a big hitter, slammed a ball straight at a bedroom window. But, just before contact, someone in the house opened the window and the ball landed on a bed. The ball was returned – with a laugh but also a warning.

The boys' only encounter with the police concerned playing cricket in the street. One day a policeman, on his bike, was riding up the main road and then made a detour to the street. This was because – he said in court – he could hear a noise in the street. They knew this couldn't possibly have been the case, and rightly surmised that a neighbour had made a complaint. The policeman told them this later, but didn't say who was responsible. Their mothers accompanied them to the juvenile court and asked the magistrates where the boys were supposed to play. A lengthy discussion took place about the playing facilities in the area, and the case was dismissed. They each had to pay five shillings 'costs of court'. Speculation was rife as to who had reported them to the police. The boys unanimously decided on the culprit. Their parents argued with them that he was a very nice man and it probably wasn't him. But the boys would have none of this. Many years later the truth came out and the boys were shown to be wrong.

North Dene was two miles from Barnfield, and two miles from the nearest coal mine. When Ken was a boy the only other houses nearby were Burn Top – a quadrangle of terraced cottages – and a few owner-occupied detached houses and bungalows on the road to Bradstone, which was the nearest pit village.

The cottages of Burn Top, being very old, had middens for lavatories – a midden being a circular drum about four feet high, with a wooden plank across the top with a hole in the middle. The doors didn't reach from top to bottom, and when someone was using the midden the lower parts of their legs were visible and also their heads. Some fascinating conversations were held between the occupiers and the passers-by, but they tended to be short because of the accompanying odour. Men came round, once a week, with a lorry to empty the middens.

The centre of the quadrangle was surfaced with ashes, and was a wonderful setting for bonfires on November the fifth. Each year the children of North Dene and Burn Top competed to see who could make the biggest bonfire. Burn Top won every year. The North Dene children complained that they had further to fetch the 'bunny-wood'. The woods were that bit nearer to Burn Top. It wasn't really a good enough excuse. Fathers' saws and axes were used to fell the trees, and they cut them into pieces which six or seven boys could manage to carry using short strong pieces to support the log. They worked like ants, starting towards the end of the summer holidays. Once a lot of wood had been collected, storage was difficult because of space and also security. Protecting your own and trying to steal the others' was as much fun as cutting down and fetching and carrying the wood home. The excitement mounted as the big day approached, because the fear was that on bonfire night eve they would be out-manœuvred and be left with little wood for the fire the next day. North Dene rarely came out second best at this – but even so, never had the biggest bonfire. The children from the detached houses did join them in these activities, but only spasmodically.

How North Dene and Burn Top had arisen was difficult to make out, because they were built in the middle of farmers' fields, meadow land, fern woods and forests; a lovely environment for any child to be brought up in.

The infant and junior schools were together, a mile away, and a school bus took the children to and fro each day. All the children, except for the odd one or two who went to a private school, attended these schools. The secondary schools, serving the children of North Dene and

Burn Top won every year.

Burn Top, were in Barnfield – separate grammar schools for boys and girls, a mixed central and a mixed secondary modern school. Children who passed the eleven plus examination went to the grammar schools; those who almost passed, to the central school; and the remainder to the secondary modern. A little movement at this stage did occur; a child who did well, after a year or two, could move up. Also, there was a technical school, and children who wished to take the subjects taught there had to pass an examination at the age of thirteen in order to gain entry. Often, some of these later entered grammar school sixth forms.

On the whole Ken had enjoyed his school life, but some things he hadn't enjoyed – like the smack he received from his mother when he arrived home after the first day. He walked into the living room and announced, 'I'm off upstairs for a piss, Mam.' She smacked him first, then said, 'You've never heard that word in this house.' Ken was shocked and aggrieved. 'All the lads at school say it.' 'Well, you don't say it in here. Now go and have a pee-wee.'

School caps were another source of embarrassment. His mother had told him, when he got his first one, that he must always take it off when he went indoors. They then went to Bradstone Co-op Grocery Store as they usually did on a Friday after school, and he took off his cap when they entered the shop. It was a big shop and all the assistants, whom he knew quite well, had a good laugh at his expense. Ken went bright red and put his cap back on.

One week he missed the Saturday morning picture show he usually went to in Barnfield, and decided to go to one at Royworth, a village just three miles away, which had a children's matinée in the afternoon. He didn't know what time it started, not having been there before, so he set off in good time. He was much too early – the first there in fact. The doorman told him where to stand to start a queue. Slowly the queue formed but, with fifteen minutes

153

to go before the doors were opened, three boys, obviously locals and bigger than he, approached him and looked him up and down. His new cap seemed to be the focus of most of their attention. They didn't say anything, but one of them removed it to inspect it more closely. Having done this he then skimmed it to the back of the queue, saying, 'Follow thi cap.' Ken made no reply and went to the back of the queue and picked up his cap. The three boys remained at the front of the queue. Ken enjoyed the show, but not as much as when he went with his pals to Barnfield.

The bus he and his friends caught to junior school in the mornings, after dropping them off, took the secondary school children into Barnfield. Some of the Grammar School boys – prefects they were (he learned later) – wore caps with a tassel. Ken's friend Tony would insist that, if you pulled the tassel, a bell rang. One day Tony decided to put this to the test. When the bus stopped for them to get off they had to push past a boy who was standing in the aisle. Tony was in front of Ken, and as he passed yanked the tassel and ran. The prefect didn't know what was happening and the lady bus conductor clipped Tony around the ear and gave the cap back to its owner. As Tony and Ken were always together she gave Ken a clip as well, just for good measure, as he left the bus. The prefect was still at the Grammar School when they both went there the following year, but they kept well out of his way. He was kind to them, because he never mentioned the incident – but he no doubt remembered them.

When Tony and Ken became prefects, tassels were still in fashion; but they stuffed their caps in their pockets until within about fifty yards of the school. They were reported on one occasion for not wearing their caps at all times, but the headmaster only ticked them off and told them to wear them in future. They complied with his request for a couple of days, then returned to their usual practice.

. . . if you pulled the tassel, a bell rang.

You sometimes got the cane at junior school, but if you did you knew that it was deserved. Skating on thin ice on a nearby pond one winter, after having been warned no to do so, was one occasion. The boys felt it was unfair because they got three of the best on both hands, whereas the girls got one gentle slap.

The sport was most enjoyable at junior school, especially when some of the teachers joined in, in the playground. If a teacher was batting at cricket the boys tried extra hard to bowl him out. You could live on that for a week. Or, if you could dispossess one when he was dribbling the ball when playing football, you got a piece of toast from Miss Tindall, an older teacher who liked watching these games. Miss Tindall kept the pieces of toast in a white cloth, and awarded them to pupils for scholastic and sporting success. The boys at their school seemed sporting daft; and the girls didn't get much toast for their sporting prowess, though they did for school work.

In fact the girls did tend to be ignored by the boys. They did, that is, until the 'bumps' started to appear in the final year. 'Bumps' had embarrassed Ken. When he was seven or eight years old, and their house was full of friends and neighbours, someone remarked how tall Ken was growing. Ken, in response, immediately went across to his mother, who was standing at the other side of the room, and measured himself against her. He stood in front of her, put his hand on top of his head, and said, 'Look, I just come up to my mam's bumps.' He couldn't understand the resultant outburst of laughter from everybody in the room. When he was eleven, and the bumps started to appear at school, he began to understand the earlier incident about bumps.

Barnfield Grammar School, in 1952, had many attractions for Ken, Tony and Ray, but again sport was the main one. Three football pitches, two cricket fields and a rugby field, all in first class condition; they were thrilled by

156

He couldn't understand the outburst of laughter.

them. The teaching staff seemed to them a gang of old eccentrics. Later they realized why this was the case. The headmaster they liked – but he himself was a little eccentric and he seemed to choose a few eccentrics like himself (but not all, of course) as his staff. Also, many of the younger teachers had been conscripted for the war and had never returned. Towards the end of their time there the balance was slowly changing, with some of the older ones retiring and young recruits taking their place.

The stories about the older ones were endless. There was a geography master who, each lesson, spent half the time writing on the blackboard, in massive capital letters, NEXT WEEK THERE WILL BE A GRAND TEST. The rest of the lesson was spent telling them what it would be about and which pages in the text book they had to learn. Come the following week, he had usually forgotten all about it, and if he did remember they got him talking about one of his pet subjects so that not many of those grand tests ever took place. Somehow, though – surprisingly – they did learn quite a lot of geography that year.

When, in the third year, chemistry was on the time-table, they got a bit excited. 'Experiments at last', they thought, but for the first few lessons they were disappointed; only theory and text books seemed to be used. But one day, when they went into the laboratory, on the bench at the front of the class was a bunsen burner and a tripod. On the tripod was a gauze square, impregnated with asbestos, and on this was a beaker half-filled with a colourless liquid. The teacher entered, lit the burner and started to heat the liquid. He allowed the liquid to boil and then cool a little. He then took a white packet from his pocket, took out a tablet of some kind, and dropped it in. He stirred with a glass rod until it was dissolved. Then he picked up the beaker and drank the contents. He put away the tripod and beaker, muttering to himself something about indigestion. A few lessons later he again got out the beaker and tripod, but on this occasion didn't say anything about indigestion.

A history teacher had a habit of spending the whole lesson reading large chunks to them from a text book. His discipline was not all that it should have been, and the boys usually did their maths homework during his lessons. Half-way through a lesson a cheeky but enterprising boy, sitting right under his desk on the front row, stopped him in full flow and asked him a question. The teacher stopped reading and addressed himself to the question in the maths textbook the boy passed to him. He studied it for a while, said it was a long time since he had done any maths and could not help, passing, as he said this, the book back to the boy. The boy turned round and asked the boy behind him if he could help. By this time the teacher had resumed reading, oblivious to the fact that not one of the boys in the class was listening to him. The teacher was nearing retirement and, after a school inspection, was allowed to go with dignity, having completed forty years' service. His discipline had not always been a problem. Only towards the end did he start to lose control. The school had a high sporting reputation, excelling at soccer, cricket and athletics.

17

THE BOYS IN KEN'S STREET also loved sport. His parents
liked most sports, and had encouraged him to take part.
He had first been taken, by them, to watch Barnfield F.C.
when he was only three years old. His father had perched
him on his shoulders so that he could see the game. During the first half, Ken had kept asking to be taken to the
lavatory to wee. His father was too interested in the
match. Half way through the second half, Ken's father had
turned to his mother and said that his back felt wet and
warm. Ken could not remember this happening, but was
reminded about it, in company and to his embarrassment,
for years to come. It did not stop them going to the games,
but his requests had been listened to after that.

Often, too, his mother would meet him after junior
school and they would go to the pictures together. They
would have a cup of tea, sandwiches, and buns in Wool-
worths first, and then go on to the pictures. His father
could not go because he was working nights and had to
rest in preparation. Walt Disney films such as *Bambi* and
Snow White and the Seven Dwarfs were favourites, as were
musicals with stars such as Fried Astaire and Ginger Rog-
ers, Doris Day and Debbie Reynolds. Ken particularly
remembered *Tom Brown's Schooldays*, especially the
scene when Tom was kidded to bend over and one of the
other boys kicked him up the backside. 'They kicked me
up the arse sir,' he had said to the headmaster when
questioned about it. This had really tickled Ken.

Without fail the boys went to the Saturday morning
children's show at the Regal cinema in town. They
enjoyed cowboys and Indians films, and Flash Gordon
serials, the most. Deciding who played which part in the
afternoon in the streets caused many arguments when the

. . . so that he could see the game.

re-enactments took place. They usually decided to take turns playing the best part.

Being a collier, his father always took Ken and his mother to the Annual Yorkshire Miners' Gala. Sometimes it was held in Barnfield, at other times in Doncaster, Wakefield or Leeds. How he enjoyed helping to push the banner of his father's pit, his only regret being that he didn't know many of the other children there because he did not live in Bradstone. Pushing the banner, and all the exciting entertainments after the march, were ample compensation though. How proud his mother and father felt on those days. They put on their Sunday best and enjoyed every moment of the walk in the procession behind the banner. His father listened attentively to the speeches that followed, but by that time Ken had made friends, was enjoying the roundabouts and coconut shies, and couldn't wait to get around to all the other stalls that were present.

Back at home in the evening, one year, his father said that he had counted one hundred and thirty people from Bradstone marching behind their banner. The Bradstone Colliery brass band had won the Best Band Competition that year. 'What a fantastic achievement', was his father's comment. His father's other comment every year was that the Yorkshire Gala could not quite match 'The Big Meeting' that the Durham miners held each year. Ken could not compare as he had never attended one of these, but he didn't really believe him.

They also attended together the annual 'Hospital Sing' at Bradstone, which was held to raise money for the Barnfield General Hospital. All the mining villages held a sing. Civic dignitaries attended, and the church and chapels helped with the organization. Hymns were sung and, after a short service in the open air, a collection was made.

Every July, when the pits closed for the holidays, the pit ponies also had a rest. But for them it was a case of 'a change is as good as a rest', for they took part in the Pit Pony Racing in the recreation ground. How Ken wanted to ride in these races, but his mother would not let him. Each pit had a horse – a shire horse which had retired from work in the pit – and this was groomed to take part in the competitions they held for them. What magnificent sights they were. Ken felt that Nugget, the Bradstone horse, was one of the family – for his father talked about him so much. At times Ken wondered however his father ever did any work at the pit, because it sounded as though he spent most of his time with the ponies in the stables. He talked to them and took them sugar lumps every day.

His mother was much the same, although in her case she collected stray cats. Ken could not remember any cat they had ever had which had been acquired in any other way than this.

Bradstone had a church with a church hall, four chapels, a picture house, swimming baths, public houses, working men's clubs and small shops of all descriptions, although the biggest and most patronized was the Barnfield Co-operative Society grocery store. A dividend was paid twice-yearly on all purchases, and this was a very effective way of saving for Christmas and summer holidays. Each member had a number which was recorded every time a sale was made. Once the children were able to count to ten, the first number they were taught was the Co-op number, so that it could be reeled off even if they were only buying a packet of sweets.

Doctors had their main surgeries in Bradstone. A big attraction for the children was the recreation ground, with swings and roundabouts for the younger children, a tennis court, bowling greens, and football and cricket pitches for the older children and adults. It was kept in beautiful condition by the local council, especially the grass and flower beds.

In addition to its other uses, the church hall was used on

163

Friday and Saturday nights for dancing. The recreation ground, the church hall for dancing, and the picture house for cuddling on the back row if you were old enough, were the main attractions for the children of North Dene and Burn Top. If you weren't old enough you watched The Three Stooges, The Bowery Boys, Gene Autrey, Tex Ritter, Doris Day, Bette Davis and all the other film stars of the time. They tended to go to Bradstone at the age of twelve for the pictures, and at sixteen for the dancing. They used the recreation ground at all ages. For the dancing a five-piece band was in attendance. When you first started going to the dances you quickly discovered who fancied who – because a boy had to ask a girl for a dance. Refusals didn't occur, because everything was done so politely. Also, 'Ladies Invitations' cropped up frequently during the evening and so the girls also had a chance to let the boys know whom they took a liking to. Life could be full of pleasant or, sometimes, not so pleasant, surprises. The girl you liked never seemed to come and ask you to dance when she had the chance, and if a boy could pluck up the courage to ask the young lady he liked the look of, usually when he was halfway across the room some other more adventurous boy nipped in and took the prize away.

Ken had made his first bumbling steps on the dance floor here – a barn dance, a nice simple one to begin with. He thought he would never learn, but with help from his mother with the steps, in their front room, he managed it. Barn dances, Valetas, Military Two-Steps, Waltzes, Foxtrots, Quicksteps and Tangos were the popular dances. The people attending were aged from sixteen to eighty, and such happy times they were, especially at Christmas. The Christmas dances were the highlight of the year. All the women baked for the Boxing Day dance; and with the decorations, food, music and dancing, nobody would have missed it for the world. At Christmas the courting instincts were put to one side – well, almost, because party games

164

were intermingled with the dancing. It was just one huge Christmas party. It wasn't a very big hall, so you had to make sure you obtained a ticket early. The regulars, rightly, had first option.

Ken had found it difficult to get to the dance on Fridays, because his father didn't approve. His father liked him to get his weekend homework out of the way. 'Don't put off till tomorrow what you can do today,' he used to advise. Dad worked regular nights at Bradstone Colliery, and had to leave home at 9.00 p.m. for a ten o'clock start. With the connivance of his mother, Ken used to catch the 9.15 p.m. bus to Bradstone. Caution had to be shown, just in case Dad happened to have missed his bus. If Ken's father found him in the front room doing his homework on Sunday, Ken made the excuse that he'd had a lot that particular weekend. To this day his father never knew of his trips to Bradstone on Friday nights, or at least he didn't think he knew.

North Dene had a church nearby, or rather a church hall which acted as an all-purpose building. It was a church on Sunday and a church hall the rest of the week. Not enough people lived near it for it to have developed the social life that you got at Bradstone. The nearest chapel was half a mile away on the road to Barnfield. Ken had at first gone to Sunday school at the church hall at North Dene, but most of his pals went to the chapel Sunday-school. He sold his soul for a shilling, or rather the chance of getting a shilling. He knew that if you passed the eleven-plus examination to go to Barnfield Grammar School the Sunday school teacher at the chapel gave you a shilling. He changed his allegiance at the age of nine to have a chance of getting the shilling, though he also wanted to be with his pals. He duly obtained the shilling, as did most of his friends.

After the Second World War, when Ken was seven and Aneurin Bevan was inaugurating the National Health Service, this environment started to change. A lot of land was needed for housing, so that as the slums in Barnfield were demolished the people could be re-housed in good housing on new estates. As the estates were built, so were shops, public houses and schools to cater for the increasing population's needs. Before, they only had two small shops, which sold just about everything. Now the Barnfield Co-operative Society had built a large grocery store and a chemist's shop at North Dene. To get a prescription dispensed before had meant a two mile trip.

The people of North Dene and Burn Top were quite taken up with all these new facilities on their doorstep. With the increase in population, the Church was even able to build a proper church, and the local girls had no need to go to Bradstone to get married. They could, even before, get married at North Dene; but they wanted the setting of a real church, lych-gate and all. This was so important for the photographs. They usually had the receptions at North Dene church hall. The vicar of North Dene didn't care much for this arrangement, but there wasn't much he could do about it.

The vicar was well-liked, if a little eccentric. He lived in Ken's street and had a habit, when walking down the street from the church hall to his home, of walking like a high-wire artist balancing on the kerbstone's edge. The local people decided that he composed his sermons when balancing like that, for he seemed completely oblivious to the rest of his surroundings. Gas-lamps were placed thirty yards apart up the street, and on occasions, when the vicar had been performing his high-wire act, he had been known to bump into one. The man who came around on a bike in the evenings to switch the lamps on with a long pole, and again in the mornings off, had told him once, jokingly, that he was going to report him to the gas office for damaging their property.

One year the vicar decided to start a Boy Scouts group,

166

and all the boys rushed to join. On the first night he produced booklets for everyone, with illustrations of all the knots that would need to be learned. He told them to practise, and that he would see how many they could perform the following week. Ken's father, having been in the Navy, knew all these knots and a few more besides. With his father's help Ken mastered every knot in the book, ready for the next meeting. At the start of the following week's meeting the vicar asked if any boy could do all the knots. Ken's hand shot up.

'Right, come up to the front and show us, Kenneth,' said the vicar.

Ken walked proudly forward. As he carefully did each knot the vicar shook his head from side to side, but didn't say anything. When he had completed them all the vicar informed him that he had only got one right, and that was the easiest of them all – the reef knot – but that the sheep-shanks, clove-hitches and the rest were all wrong. The other boys collapsed into a heap of laughter.

When Ken got home after the meeting he shouted at his father, telling him what had happened and accusing him of teaching him all the wrong knots. They went over them again. Dad was right, apparently, not the vicar. The adjective used by Ken's father to describe the vicar was not repeatable. His father didn't mention any of this to the vicar, and their relationship remained a friendly one although his father never attended church – not, that is, until he died.

At the following week's meeting the vicar asked Ken if he had practised them, and also if he had had any help with them. Ken said that he had, and mentioned the fact about his father's time in the navy. Ken then repeated all the knots exactly as he had the previous week. The vicar congratulated him on his diligence over the past week, and approved them all.

Ken's career as a boy scout didn't last long. Most of the

other boys drifted away too as they realized the vicar didn't really know much about scouting.

Ken's mother attended church occasionally, and she did support all the social activities – whist drives, beetle drives, concerts and fairs – all being necessary to raise funds to keep the church in existence. At the summer fair a local farmer used to bring along two ponies. The children were charged two pence a ride. The braver souls raced around the field which was behind the hall, and sometimes the ponies behaved like runaway trains. All the aspiring Gordon Richards had lots of rides. It was also a chance for the boys to do a bit of showing off in front of the girls.

The church hall had been built on brick stilts, so the boys (and girls, for that matter) could crawl underneath it. One year, when rain had forced everybody indoors, the boys resorted to beneath the hall. An enterprizing boy, and a bit of a rogue to boot, went home and brought back his father's drill. The floor of the hall was made of wood. By carefully pacing up and down inside the hall he worked out the exact location of the ladies' toilet. He charged the boys, assembled under the hall, threepence a peep – although the price did vary depending on who was using the toilet at the particular time it was your turn to have a look. The older the user, the lower the price; the younger and more attractive the user, the higher the price. Market forces at work. Supply and demand and all that. All the other boys dashed home to raid their money boxes. That particular year, at the end of the day, this boy took home with him more money than the farmer had raised for the church funds. He decided against donating the money to the church, because the vicar might ask him how he had obtained it. Also, he didn't wish to lose a potential source of income. This boy, on reaching manhood, and after one or two false starts, settled down as a bookmaker and became one of the richest men in town.

He worked out the exact location of the ladies' toilet.

He lived in the second of the two streets, the one behind Ken's street. The boys in that street tended to be just that bit older, and in all the competitions that took place between the two streets they usually came out on top. They competed at football, cricket, kite-flying, throwing bricks at each other, snowballing, cycle racing, speedway racing on bikes, and sundry other activities. Train-spotting had its addicts.

Each street had a leader, who did the organizing and timing of these events. In Ken's street this duty fell to a boy who was sporting mad. His enthusiasm knew no bounds, and his inventiveness was unrivalled. For the speedway racing he persuaded a farmer to let them have the use of part of one of his fields. He then organized the making of a track in this field. The boys' mothers made them colours and, for a whole year, a speedway league existed for them.

To form the league the streets, on this occasion, had to be divided into sections. Fixtures were arranged on a weekly basis, and the competition was fierce. The bikes took a mighty hammering, but they took great pride in these machines and cleaned and polished them assiduously.

18

AT THE END OF THE YEAR, when the interest began to wane, the bikes were hardly fit to carry them to the summer destinations this boy planned for them. The Peak District of Derbyshire was a popular route, Castleton and the caves being a firm favourite. To the north Knaresborough, with its castle, zoo, and river with rowing boats and punts, was within easy cycling distance. A two hour ride there, sandwiches, a rest, and perhaps an hour on the river, was followed by the journey home in the evening. They arrived tired but glowing after their day's exertion. This gave them enormous appetites, which were assuaged by cold mutton or beef and fried-up potatoes left over from the Sunday dinner.

Short time-trial cycle races, of approximately ten to twenty-five miles, were a regular pastime. Fathers' watches were procured, surreptitiously, so that times could be recorded. Cigarettes, too, were often obtained, again surreptitiously (it could be called thieving), but these didn't seem to improve the times of the riders.

Then one year a more ambitious journey was contemplated – to go and watch the finish of a stage of the first ever 'Tour of Britain'. The 'Tour de France' they had always followed, stage by stage, in *The Bicycle* magazine which came out weekly. Fausto Coppi, the great Italian rider, was Ken's hero. Fausto sat on the bike and, when the mountains arrived, he just used to ride away from the rest of the field, seemingly without much effort. Reading how he did it thrilled Ken to the core. What he would have given to be like that!

The Frenchman, Louison Bobet, was his closet rival and soon started winning the Tours. A 'Woman in White' began to appear in Fausto's life. She was reported as being spotted at the roadside during his races. Ken was disappointed to notice that Fausto was getting more interested in her than in winning the Tours of France, Spain and Italy, 'The Big Three'. Fausto's life came to a premature end at the age of about forty. When the news of his death was reported in *The Bicycle*, Ken cried. It was the first time he had ever cried when learning of the death of someone. His boyhood hero was gone. He was to cry when other sporting heroes of his died, but those were some years later.

When it was announced that a Tour of Britain was to take place, all the boys in the streets had their own favourites. They tended to favour someone they felt was like themselves. Ray, who was short and stocky, went for Dave Bedwell, the Hercules rider. Hercules, at that time, made rather ponderous cycling machines. But when it was announced that a Tour of Britain was imminent they quickly made some racing machines and signed up some of the leading riders in the country. They couldn't afford to be left out. Sales would be lost.

Sponsorship in cycling was taking off. The press and radio coverage would be comprehensive, and every time David Bedwell was mentioned it would also say that he rode for the Hercules team. He was the captain of their team.

Ken's favourite was Ian Steele, a Scot from Glasgow, six feet tall, dark-haired and very slim. Ian was captain of the Viking team. Five or six riders were thought to have a good chance of winning, but Bedwell and Steele were the two most fancied. Stan Maitland, only just turned professional, had many followers.

This first Tour went up the West of Britain, across Scotland, and down the East, finishing in London. There was not much in it to begin with as they approached the Scottish borders on the way up. The race was going, more or less, as predicted, with Bedwell and Steele near the

. . . some of the leading riders in the country.

head of the field. The stage from Carlisle to Glasgow settled the race. Going up Shap Fell, Ian Steele made his move. He was a climber par excellence in Britain, and he'd been waiting for his chance. The fact that this stage would end in his home city of Glasgow made him even more determined. He entered Glasgow to an ecstatic welcome, talked about for years, eighteen minutes in front of the second man home. Eighteen minutes! This seemed unbelievable. When Ken read about it, in the Daily Herald the following day, he was convinced it was a misprint. But no, it was right!

All he had to do now was to make no mistakes on the way back to London, and the race was his. Coming down, the Hercules team ran into trouble. Some of their riders being injured in a crash, the Hercules team manager withdrew the team. The sight of Dave Bedwell, crying, standing with his machine by the roadside when the decision was taken, made a poignant picture in *The Bicycle*. He was crying because he knew he would not be the winner of the first ever Tour of Britain.

After losing the Carlisle to Glasgow stage he'd been pulling some time back, but he knew that only an accident to Steele could give him a chance of winning. Even so, he never gave up. He wanted to go on trying to the very end. It was the manager's decision, and he had to obey. Ian Steele was the victor. Ken's wildest dreams had come true. Ian's, I suppose, too.

19

THE BOYS of North Dene and Burn Top decided to go to Stoke-on-Trent – the nearest the Tour came to Barnfield. It would be a round trip of one hundred and forty miles. They had never attempted a distance of that magnitude before. It was daunting, but they were determined to have a go. Their mothers didn't like the sound of it, but their fathers thought it would be alright.

'Going to the Five Towns, are you?' Ken's mother remarked when he showed her the route.

'No, Stoke-on-Trent.'

'Don't they teach you these things at school?' The potteries were known as The Five Towns. I've been listening to a serial on the wireless, called *Anna of the Five Towns*, about that area.

Fortunately, that day's stage was on a Sunday. They planned it down to the minutest detail. The day dawned and it was raining cats and dogs. One or two didn't show up. Later they complained that their parents would not let them go because of the weather. They had pleaded to be allowed to go, but to no avail. The others did not believe them, and during the next week were not charitable. 'Chicken', they were called. 'I'll ask thi' mam and dad,' said one, threatening exposure of the truth.

They donned their yellow oilskins and caps, and set off. They were not sure if the bikes were up to such a long journey. Money was scarce, and their bikes were known as ABCs – 'All Bits Combined' – a bit from here, a bit from there, a pair of 'drop' racing handlebars for Christmas, a derailleur gear saved up for with weekly pocket money, toe-clips for a birthday. Nine months it had taken Ken to save up for the Simplex gear.

Only Ray had a smashing bike. He managed to get a job

on Saturdays at a bike shop in town, and instead of getting paid the manager let him build his own bike. He started with just a frame, and then custom-built it. He learned how to make wheels and balance them, and everything that was to be known about a bike. He proved to be a great asset to them in the street. Also, he could get discount on spare parts.

After two miles they decided to stop under a railway bridge to shelter. In spite of the oilskins they were already soaked to the skin. A flash of lightning rent the sky. A discussion about whether to continue ensued. Pros and cons. Every one of them probably wanted to suggest going home, back to a nice warm bed. Even now it was only 7.00 a.m. – it needed an early start to get there in time to see the finish. No one wanted to be the one to make the proposal. If someone had made the suggestion and it had been acted upon his life would not have been worth living for the next year. 'If it hadn't been for you we wouldn't have turned back,' the others would have rebuked him at every opportunity, forgetting that they had acquiesced in the decision.

So on they went. The wind and rain didn't let up. Sheffield, Ladybower (with its submerged village) and to Castleton where they stopped for a sandwich and a cup of tea. Again, talk of going home; but again no one was prepared to make the first move.

About two miles out of Buxton, it happened. Ray, normally a strong rider who usually had no problems keeping with the pace, had been struggling since Castleton. He had had a heavy cold the previous week. They took turns in going to the front, with the rest taking in behind to have a breather. When it was realized that Ray was having problems it was agreed, unanimously, that he should always stay at the back to try and conserve his energy.

Turning a corner his concentration lapsed, and he hit

176

the back wheel of the rider in front of him. When this happens it is the rider at the back who comes the cropper. The others heard the crash and immediately pulled up. Ray seemed to have blood coming from everywhere, but it was not as bad as it looked. They soon cleaned him up and put antiseptic and plasters on the cuts and grazes. Each one of them carried first-aid material in his saddle-bag. The bike was a different matter – the front wheel bent and one of the pedals twisted. The situation looked hopeless, but they had forgotten about Ray's knowledge of bikes. After recovering from the shock he quickly got the bike serviceable again. The others couldn't have done it, but Ray did. And although the bike couldn't be ridden as smoothly as before, he could go on.

Once more, talk of going back.

'Look, if I can carry on as before, at the back, if that suits you lads, I want to get to Stoke,' said Ray.

So on they pushed. This had delayed them an hour. Almost there now. A great cheer went up as they passed the Stoke City boundary sign at the side of the road.

Into Stoke itself. But delays as they made enquiries and were directed to the part of the city in which the stage was due to finish. A woman sent them, as they realized later, in the wrong direction. Her parentage was put to some scrutiny in the days to follow. Eventually they found the spot. They were dismayed. Cars carrying bikes on top of them were driving away, spectator cyclists were riding away, and all the pedestrians who had gathered for the finish were dispersing. The boys could not believe their eyes.

'I can't see any of the riders,' one said.

Ray then saw a rider whose face he recognized from the photographs in *The Bicycle*. Bob Maitland's there, look,' he shouted excitedly.

Quickly they all turned and saw him. Their faces dropped even further. He was standing on the steps of a hotel

177

which was situated just beyond the day's finishing line. He had a quick word with someone, signed a couple of autographs, and disappeared into the hotel.

They just could not believe it. Not another rider was to be seen. They were bitterly disappointed to have missed the finish, but a lot of compensation would have been theirs if they could have just looked at the riders in their racing clothes and colours, and at the bikes. The men and the bikes; that was what they wanted to look at. Stare at them, inspect them, touch them if possible. They wanted to see what sort of tyres they used, what shape the saddle was, the type of gears. Handlebars too were so important – the shape of them, where the brakes were positioned to aid the hill climbing when standing on the pedals, out of the saddle. The make of the brake was fascinating. Have a look and try to copy later. These were the experts – they must know how to choose all this equipment and position it to produce the best results because, after all, they had risen to the top of this magical sport of cycle-racing.

But, of course, it was the top riders they especially wanted to see. The men. Just to see them, to catch a snatch of conversation, to see how they looked after six hours in the saddle averaging almost twenty-five miles an hour. They never quite looked as you imagined. They were either shorter or taller, fatter or thinner.

Ken had once seen Ian Steele in a one day race around the Peak District and Sheffield. Ken could not quite take in how thin he was. However does that frame and those legs win all those races? There is hope for me yet, he thought. If only they could have seen them, it would have given them material to talk about for hours in the weeks to come. How could you talk for hours about Bob's back disappearing into a hotel? No disrespect to Bob of course. He was a firm favourite of theirs, way back from his days as the top amateur rider. His autograph would have been something, but they could not get across the road in time to get even that.

Nobody spoke. The wind was still howling, and the rain lashed down. But for the weather, they felt they would have seen the riders. Normally they hung about for a while, but today the rain had driven them inside. They would want warm drinks, food, and a hot bath. No such luxuries awaited the boys in Stoke. It was now three o'clock, and seventy miles back to Barnfield wasn't a happy prospect for them. They had been warned by their parents not to be late home, because it was school the following day.

20

THESE SEVEN THIRTEEN-YEAR-OLDS found a cafe in which to eat the sandwiches their mothers had packed the night before and to get some tea. They heaped as much sugar into the tea as was possible. One of them had read somewhere that sugar was energy, and they all knew that they were going to need plenty of that. They asked the woman behind the counter if she could refill their water bottles, as most of them had been emptied on the journey to Stoke. This she did readily. What must she have thought, looking at these bedraggled youths? They were drying out a bit now, but they were mud-splattered and dejected-looking. When she was in a back room they put the sugar from all the bowls on the tables into their bottles. As they ate and drank the tea their spirits lifted somewhat. It had to be faced – the journey back – and soon.

Tactics. That's what they had to discuss now. The preparations for this ride had been thorough. The bikes had been given a lot of attention and polished, although the latter had soon proved a waste of time because of the foul weather. Even so, it had not been a complete waste of time, because it had given them confidence.

They had trained to a schedule for the previous three weeks. Ten to fifteen miles every evening, thirty to forty miles every Saturday and Sunday. They were fitter than they had ever been. Every one of them had improved on his best ever time over the ten-mile time-trial course they had devised. They could not believe how their times had got better whilst following this schedule. They knew all this, but the doubts persisted. Ninety miles in a day was the most any of them had ever achieved. This was a lot, lot, more than that.

'Take it at an even pace,' one said. 'Don't rush at it and

They were mud-splattered and dejected-looking.

get "the bonk".'

This was the word nobody wanted to mention, but it had slipped out. They all knew about 'the bonk', and each one of them had been thinking about it. None of them had ever experienced it. How many times had they read about riders in the Tour de France getting 'the bonk'? Even the best riders got it sometimes. It could strike out of a clear blue sky. You were OK one minute, going along fine and up with the leaders, then wham! – it could hit you. Your legs, apparently, went like jelly. Not an ounce of energy left. Inside minutes you dropped off the pace, caught by the chasing pack, then not even able to stay with the pack. Minutes earlier – thoughts of winning the race. Now – will I even finish it? They all suffered and sympathized with riders who got 'the bonk' – so unfair it seemed. No justice in the world. They had trained, looked after themselves, done nothing wrong – so why had it hit them? Actors on first nights did not mention *Macbeth*; racing cyclists **never** mentioned 'The Bonk'. How could they know how to avoid the dreaded 'bonk'? The experts could not even do this. Was there any point in even talking about it, in that case?

'Shut up,' snapped Tony, when the word was uttered.

'I'm sorry. It just came out.'

Another thing they all knew was that the wind would be against them all the way back. They had planned a different route back to avoid one or two big hills, but could not avoid the hills that came in the last ten miles after Sheffield. Not particularly steep ones, but a lot of them. They took these in their stride on their training rides, but anticipating them now after riding 130 miles, they looked a different kettle of fish.

'There's nothing to be served by not talking about it. We might come up with something. It's daft not talking about it,' said Ken.

'We've plenty of fruit and sugar-lumps left,' another

182

one said, trying to lift the spirits.

'Well said,' said Ken.

'Doesn't make any difference, we all know that,' snarled Tony.

Ray had gone very quiet, and did not look as though he could ride one mile – let alone seventy.

'What about you, Ray?' asked Ken. 'Feeling any better now you've had a bite and a drink?'

'A bit, thanks Ken.'

'We've done the training, we'll be OK,' the cheery one said.

'The pros have all done the training, haven't they,' said Tony, very irritated by now. 'And they get it.'

'Look, Tony, he's only trying to help. Leave off. How are you feeling – rough or what? Is that the trouble?' asked Ken.

'It isn't,' he replied indignantly. 'I'm fine. I'm just trying to get myself into the right frame of mind, that's all, and all this talk of "the bonk" isn't helping.'

Tony desperately wanted to win the North Dene Tour of Britain of 1950. Ray looked as though he'd spoiled all that. The race didn't look as though it would take place now. Tony knew that they had to get Ray home somehow, and was feeling very irritated. It was not that he did not like Ray. He did. It was just that he wanted the race to take place.

Every Sunday trip they had ever been on had turned into a race. Nice and leisurely going out, but it was silently acknowledged that for the last twenty miles coming home the race started proper. Going out and coming back they had 'King of the Sprints' over town and city boundary lines, and 'King of the Mountains' contests on any hill they thought arduous enough. That is why they regularly went into Derbyshire. The reservoir at Ladybower, the caves at Castleton, were attractions; but it was the hills they really went for – none of them the same.

The long seven-mile trek up the Rivelyn Valley from Sheffield – not steep in any place, but the slow drag sorted them out. Then sweeping down to Ladybower and down again to Castleton for a rest before tackling the mighty Mam Tor on the road to Chapel-en- le-Frith. This was the best test they had ever found. Long, twisting, winding – getting steeper by the yard. This was their 'Col D'Aspin' they so much loved reading about.

Whoever crossed the top first was the undisputed 'King of the Mountains'. All of them had won it on occasions, but Tony the most. They didn't keep a record of the score, but they all knew it. On these trips they always re-grouped after the sprints and climbs and helped each other – that is until the last twenty miles. Then it was every man for himself. And this was the one, secretly, they all wanted to win. Each of them fancied his chances – except Ray, who was downcast as he thought his chance had gone. He felt he would make it home, barring another accident. But win? No chance now.

The other six were weighing each other up. They would be entering new territory. Each of them was trying to remember something similar to this so that they could compare performances. No use. The next longest trips to this had been one through York and another to Lincoln; but they were very flat runs, and couldn't be compared with this.

Ken thought he understood Tony's state of mind. He too was wondering how he could win, but his approach for concentrating the mind was different. Let's all talk about it; any idea might help everybody. He wanted them all back in one piece. But he did want to win. No doubt about that. He knew that if they discussed it an idea might crop up that he hadn't thought of, and this might help him win. Tony knew Ken very well, and that's why he kept quiet. Ken, he had calculated, was the biggest danger. He knew he could beat him eight times out of ten on Mam Tor. Ken wasn't the greatest of climbers, but he also knew that Ken was the group's best time-trialist; on your own against the clock. 'The Race of Truth', it was called. Ken was almost unbeatable in time trials. Tony knew that he couldn't, mustn't, daren't, under-estimate Ken.

This journey, he knew, he wouldn't be worried about. It had been Ken's idea, in the first place, to go to Stoke – and Tony knew why. They just had to find out, and this was a suitable test. Tony had felt comfortable all the way to Stoke, but he had noticed that Ken had cruised there as well. He watched him carefully all the time; but no comfort there. Two of the others also looked very relaxed, but their track record didn't suggest they would be a serious challenge. 'Good steady plodders,' he thought, 'but inconceivable that they could win. Must keep an eye on them though,' he reminded himself, glancing around the table and searching their faces. He didn't look at Ken; he knew it would be a waste of time. He gave nothing away. He was sorry about Ray's accident on two counts – genuinely sorry that he was not well and had crashed, but mainly because he thought Ray would have made it a hell of a race, possibly drawing Ken out at the finish and leaving Tony to come from the back to win. This had happened before. Ray took risks, calculated risks, but nevertheless risks. He would have a go for home from a long way out because he hardly ever won a sprint finish. Sometimes he burnt himself out too soon, but if he got his timing right he was hard to catch. Judging the right time to go in a situation like this would have been very difficult for him, but Tony knew he would certainly have had a go if they were still together with ten miles left, and if he was still feeling strong. Ray had guts, he knew that. What a pity circumstances had contrived in this way.

The woman in the cafe asked them where they were from, and looked incredulous when she heard the answer. She wished them all the best and waved them off. They

185

had stiffened up, but were soon back into a good easy rhythm. In fact Ray was riding very comfortably now and insisted on helping out at the front occasionally.

Their first stop was Buxton, at a transport cafe. Ray announced that he was feeling fine, and from now on would shoulder his share of the work. Tony's face lit up at this news. The race was back on now, with a vengeance. They had made good time to Buxton, and this had really boosted them all. They agreed to stop again for another rest on the outskirts of Sheffield, and also decided that a 'King of the Mountains' contest should take place on the hill taking them from Ladybower to the top of the Rivelyn Valley – a three-mile climb.

Earlier they had decided that no sprints or mountain top contests were to take place, as this would waste energy. But so good were they feeling now, they thought that the odd one would be alright. On the climb up to Ladybower, from Bamford, Ken struggled to stay in touch at the back. He thought that only Tony had realized this. Nothing was said. He recovered a little on the flat stretch near Lady-bower, but 'the bonk' got him on the big pull to the Rivelyn top. Tony, sensing his predicament, attacked almost immediately at the bottom of the climb, and together with Ray and two of the others quickly opened a gap of thirty yards. Tony easily sprinted clear at the top, followed by the other three together, and then they stopped to wait. Ken, helped by the other two, struggled up five minutes later.

'It's not the bonk, surely?' said Ray.

'It looks like it,' said Ken, dejectedly. 'I was fine till Bamford, but then, all of a sudden, I felt drained. Come on, let's keep it going.'

They coasted down the Rivelyn valley to the agreed resting point. Ken's bonk was discussed. Ken knew that he was out of the race. Only a night's rest could improve things.

'I'll get home all right, but slowly,' he said.

They nursed him along until five miles from home. Realizing that he could amble along and would get home, they upped the pace into the final stretch. Two plodders, Tony and Ray, were soon on their own. The other two plodders stayed with Ken, although they did have enough energy left to go at a quicker pace than his. Ken urged them to join the race, but they insisted on staying with him.

Three hills were between the four breakaways and the finishing line. This was the Barnfield town boundary, situated at the top of a long steep incline. Tony assumed rightly that, because of his crash, Ray would not have a go on his own. Ray, again rightly, thought that Tony would try to crack them on the first two hills and was determined to let Tony do much of the work both approaching them and climbing them. They were both surprised that the two plodders were still in touch, especially after the first climb when Tony powered it on.

They approached the penultimate one, still all together. Tony again spurted, but only one of the plodders was dropped. Having expected to have left them all by now he eased right off to recover and assess. On the relatively flat stretch to the final hill they slowed considerably to gather themselves. Tony was still confident and felt good. Just being in with a chance at this stage boosted Ray's confidence. The plodder had trained very hard and wasn't surprised to be still with them.

Tony attacked early, but Ray stuck with him. The plodder couldn't keep up with the extra pace. Tony attacked again but only stole two or three yards on Ray, who slowly hauled it back and then himself attacked immediately. Tony fastened onto his back wheel, and with the finish one hundred yards away had another go. But Ray was equal to it and held him off by half a wheel's breadth. As they crossed the line, huge grins spread across their faces. They

187

pulled up to wait for the others. Ken's group crawled to them ten minutes later.

'Who won?' they asked, almost in unison. They were surprised but delighted by the answer. North Dene was now just half a mile away, and they rode home together singing their favourite riding song, 'We'll be coming round the mountains when we come'. Ray's victory was much talked about in the following week, but Ken's bonk was, also. They all seemed fascinated to find out just what it was like, going through the bonk.

Their winter activities were dictated by the weather. Sledging and skating on a local pond if ice and snow were in abundance. If confined to the house, fretwork, helping make clippie rugs, and listening to the wireless were the pastimes. The radio programmes were also the source of ideas for their outdoor games. *Children's Hour*, with Uncle Mac, *Dick Barton, Special Agent* and *Paul Temple* were never missed. Likewise comedy shows such as *Ignorance is Bliss* and Tommy Handley's *ITMA*. *Sports Report* with Eammon Andrews, and the broadcasts of the soccer internationals with Raymond Glendenning, climaxing with the England versus Scotland match, were compulsive listening. In these matches a shiver went up Ken's spine when Raymond said, in his own inimitable style, 'And the ball goes out to Tom Finney on the right wing.' Finney had a habit of running the Scots ragged.

The only broadcast Ken could hardly bear to listen to was on the night Bruce Woodcock, the heavyweight from Doncaster, fought the American Joe Baksi. He felt Baksi was killing him, and covered up his ears. But to put against that was the night Randolph Turpin beat Sugar Ray Robinson. It seemed to be the only time he had heard the inter-round summariser Barrington Dalby get a bit excited.

The boys did play games with the girls in the street, more in the winter when they gathered under the gas lamps to play hide-and-seek, kick-can and Jack-Jack shine-your-light. As they got older the hide-and-seeks degenerated into a farce when pairs of girls and boys tended to get lost for unusually long periods of time.

Jack, Jack, Shine-a-Light

21

Blaydon Races

Aw went to Blaydon Races, 'twas on the ninth of Joon,
 Eiteen hundred an' sixty-two, on a summer's afternoon
Aw tyuk the 'bus frae Balmbra's, an' she wis heavy laden,
 Away we went alang Collingwood Street, that's on the
  road to Blaydon.

Chorus:

  O lads, ye shud only seen us gannin'
  Passin' the foaks upon the road just as they wor
   stannin';
  Thor wes lots o' lads an' lasses there, aall wi'
   smilin' faces,
  Gannin' alang the Scotswood Road, to see the
   Blaydon Races.

We flew past Airmstrong's factory, and up to the Robin
 Adair,
 Just gannin' doon te the railway bridge, the bus wheel
  flew off there.
The lasses lost their crinolines off, an' the veils that hide
 their faces,
 An' aw got two black eyes an' a broken nose in gannin'
  te Blaydon Races.

When we gat the wheel put on away we went agyen,
 But them that had their noses broke, they came back
  over hyem;
Sum went to the Dispensary, an' sum to Doctor Gibbs,
 An' sum to the Infirmary, to mend their broken ribs.

Noo when we gat to Paradise thor wes bonny gam begun,
    Thor wes fower and twenty on the bus man, hoo they
        danced an' sung;
They called on me to sing a sang, aw sung them *Paddy
Fagan*,
    Aw danced a jog an' swung me twig that day aw went to
        Blaydon.

We flew across the Chain bridge, reet into Blaydon toon,
    The bellman he was caallin' there caal him Jacky Broon,
Aw saw him talking to sum chaps, an' them he was
    persuadin'
    To gan an' see Geordy Ridley's concert in the
        Mechanic's Haal at Blaydon.

The rain it pour'd aw the day an' myed the groond quite
    muddy,
    Coffy Johnny had a white hat on – they wor shootin'
        'Whe stole the cuddy'.
There were spice stalls, an' munkey shows, an' wives
    selling ciders,
    An' a chep wiv a happeny roond about shootin' 'Noo me
        lads, for riders'.

Adam and Hannah Longstaff came to Blaydon reluc-
tantly. They had both worked on the land, but the
impending birth of their third child, Martha, forced Adam
to seek employment, for economic and health reasons, in
the coal mines. They made an odd looking couple, him six
feet three inches tall – a gentle giant of a man – and her
five feet only. Looking after a family and also working
long hours in the fields was the only way they could make
ends meet, but her health was beginning to suffer.

Though poor, they were happy – living and working on
the rich farmlands of Richmond, North Yorkshire. They
managed to find a home on the outskirts of Blaydon,
which enabled them to compromise. Summer Hill was a
short terrace of small cottages on the top of a hill, with
plenty of land for each of the occupants. They were thus
able to keep pigs and hens, and cultivate their own

vegetables and fruit. His pipe, a pint, and his smallholding, kept him content.

Adam was apprehensive about becoming a collier; not particularly about going underground, although this was a factor, but mainly because of the reputation of the mining communities, for they were still regarded in some quarters as a people apart and an inferior race; even, in fact, as sub-human. His fears on both scores were soon dispelled. He quickly adapted to the work at the coal face, finding the men comradely and friendly and the whole community supportive of one another. Hannah found the transition more difficult, but gradually settled down with the help of the local priest. Her family had moved from Ireland in the middle of the nineteenth century. Her fair freckled face and ginger hair bore testimony to her ancestry.

Nine children were born to them, a boy dying in the first year of life leaving five girls and three boys. Two of the boys followed their father into the mines, and the other found work in a nearby shipyard. Three of the girls went into service. Martha got a job in the Shoe Department of Blaydon Co-operative Society, and the eldest stayed at home to look after the house and her ailing mother. Nine children in sixteen years of married life had taken its toll, and she was confined to the house with a failing heart.

Hannah being a Roman Catholic, the children attended the church school, and mass every Sunday. When, at the age of fourteen, Martha left school, she abruptly stopped going to church and ignored in the street her former schoolmistress. Together, the priest and teacher visited the Longstaffs to find out the reason.

'Now I'm fourteen I don't have to go and I won't,' Martha told them. Her mother was deeply upset.

'Why?' they asked.

Martha explained that she had hated the school and particularly the religious part of it – the hell-fire and damnation ideas that were thrust at them. Her family, the

193

teacher, and priest, had no previous intimation that this was how she had felt. No amount of persuading could change her mind. When her brothers or sisters visited her in later years when she lived in South Yorkshire, the first thing they used to ask was the time of the mass at church. Martha never accompanied them.

A brother, Elijah, was killed, aged sixteen, in a pit disaster. He was one of ten men who were thrown out of the cage and fell to a depth of two hundred feet. A sister, Maria, succombed to consumption in her tenth year. The others prospered to adulthood. The warm clean comfortable cottage, and the home-grown food, were obviously big factors in their survival.

22

THE APPLEYARDS arrived in Blaydon at about the same time, but lived in the town itself. The houses were back-to-backs, with no gardens, and the streets built military-style in parallel lines. Cornelius Appleyard had been a glass-blower in the Rotherham area, but had moved north in search of work as a general labourer in the dockyards. His wife Isabella was pleased to do so, as she had originated in the north and was pleased to move nearer to her relatives. Their first-born child was Ben, and not till the seventh child did a girl appear. Two more boys completed their family. Football and music was their forte. Cornelius could play the piano and taught them all to sing, and also taught Lucy how to play the piano like himself. All the boys became miners, but Lucy didn't go out to work. Football got two of them out of the pits. John was signed as a professional by Gateshead, and Thomas by Sunderland. Another had to find work away from Blaydon because of his left-wing political views. Although Blaydon was one of the strongest trade union places in the country at the time, this didn't stop the management at William's pit giving him instant dismissal because of his political zeal. In the First World War George and Henry, who had together volunteered for the Eighth Battalion Northumberland Fusiliers, perished at the Dardanelles. Isabella and Lucy found solace in the massive illustrated family Bible, and also at the local Methodist chapel where they had always been regular attenders.

Ben was a bright boy, and when the time was approaching for him to leave school his teacher, a Mr Townend, visited the Appleyards.

'I wouldn't like to see him have to go into the pits,' said Mr Townend. 'He's done so well at school. As you know,

. . . in the First World War.

he passed the leaving examination a year early.'

Between them they managed to get him a job with the Co-operative Society as a bicycle errand boy to begin with, but with prospects of getting into a shop and training for management. He stuck it for a month. Without consulting his parents he found work at a local pit and joined his friends, who regarded his errand boy work as strictly for 'cissies'. His mother was very annoyed, but he was adamant. He was called up and joined the navy two weeks after the start of the war, aged eighteen. After four years he returned to civilian life, but work in he pits was hard to come by. Even when it was available it tended to be spasmodic, and that's how he missed another opportunity in his life (the one mentioned earlier being with the book-maker).

It was at this time that he occasionally supplemented his meagre income in the local institute. He had a remarkable memory, and tests were devised to challenge him. He took bets from the other men on whether he could pass these tests. A popular one was for him to listen to all the football league results as they were announced on a Saturday afternoon. He was allowed to listen to them once only and then was asked any result at random. More often than not his winnings allowed him to go out on a Saturday evening. It was in this period that he first met Martha Longstaff.

'I've just seen a smashing girl in the shoe shop. Do you know who it is?' he asked his mother.

'The dark haired one, who smiles a lot, do you mean?'

'Yes, that's her.'

'It's Adam and Hannah Longstaff's lass. She's been working there about two or three years now. She seems a lovely girl.'

'It was love at first sight on his part, but it took him a good while to make her take much notice of him. But he persevered, and they started courting and were married three years later.

197

23

THEIR EARLY MARRIED LIFE had to be spent in lodgings, which they didn't care for at all. But it was Hobson's choice. Ben's work was becoming increasingly hard to obtain and eventually, in their second year of marriage, dried up altogether. Unemployment pay was fifty shillings a week, and the dole office informed him that that would cease as there was employment to be had in the pits in South Yorkshire. Together with a friend he cycled to Doncaster and found work at Hatfield Main Colliery, and lodgings nearby.

The working conditions were very different from what they had been used to. The heat was the problem, so they soon moved to Barnfield. Hannah refused to move to Yorkshire unless they had a house of their own. Lodgings were out of the question as far as she was concerned. Ben managed to get a month's trial at Millthorpe, where the coal company were building new houses for their employees. After two weeks the manager informed him that the trial was over and he could have one of the houses which had just been completed.

Hannah and his friend's wife and children moved to Yorkshire together. With regular work and a new house they soon settled down and adapted to their new environment. Having no children, they got through the six-month long strike of 1926 better than most. Hannah and many of the women worked for the local farmers.

It was during this period that Ben started to get more involved in the union activities at the pit. Compared to Blaydon he found the union in Yorkshire poorly organized. Barely half the men at Millthorpe were actually members of the union. He also felt that the men were encouraged to strike too readily. He wanted better wages and conditions, but the Yorkshire way of striking first and talking later he couldn't agree with. He was a regular attender at all the union meetings and argued his corner, but to no avail.

Millthorpe was a 'family pit'. The families who dominated the village life tended to dominate the pit as well. The men who held sway at the chapel and the club did so at the pit.

One year he decided to stand for election as the local union president. A vicious campaign was waged against him. VOTE FOR THE MAN WHO DIDN'T SELL HIS BIRTHRIGHT was daubed in massive letters with white paint on the pit-top buildings. The perpetrators were never found. Ben lost convincingly, and from that day was effectively ostracized by the village elders. He became sad and disillusioned with the life of Millthorpe. Before, he had spent much time in the club, often as an entertainer with his singing, but now he kept out. In fact at one point Hannah had threatened to return to Blaydon because he passed so much of his time in the club. He was pleased to leave Millthorpe and start a new life at North Dene.

PART FOUR
SOUTH YORKSHIRE – 1965

24

As ken walked towards his old school, for an interview with his former headmaster, he found himself smiling as he recollected incidents from his days spent there. One phrase of the headmaster, spoken to him as he left the stage after reading the lesson at morning assembly, kept recurring to him.

Going down the steps from the stage the headmaster had stopped and turned to Ken and said, 'Appleyard, you have disgraced a discontented cow.'

Ken had wanted to smile, because he hadn't heard that one of his before. But he managed to suppress it. They had then proceeded down the centre aisle of the school hall, out through the door at the back and into the head's study. Only prefects read the lesson, on a rota system, and this was one of the duties Ken didn't relish. Then in his seventh year at the school, he had observed this morning ritual with mounting anxiety as the years went by. He knew that if he had succeeded in getting into the sixth form he had a good chance of being made a prefect. He had represented the school at soccer and cricket, had a good academic record, and had generally not made too big a nuisance of himself to the staff. Such boys invariably became prefects. He was pleased his surname was Appleyard. This meant he would get his turn early, as the rota was arranged alphabetically. He had seen the duty performed in all sorts of ways. The boys who took part in the school plays were usually the best, taking the opportunity to give a performance. Some mumbled and stuttered, and one or two had dried up completely and had had to be led back to their chairs without completing the reading.

Ken had anticipated being competent unless nerves let him down on the day. He had not slept well the night before, but felt calm until the hymn before the reading was being sung. During this his stomach had started to churn and his heart began to thump, though he managed to control these a little before the hymn was finished. He stood up and moved towards the lectern, on which he placed the Bible.

'This morning's lesson is taken from the gospel according to St Luke, chapter nineteen, reading verses eleven to twenty-seven.' This part had come out alright, and some confidence seeped back into him. Halfway through though, his heart started to thump even more and his head was throbbing. This had a disastrous effect on the speed at which he read. He became like a runaway train. He didn't slow down until he closed the Bible and said, 'Here endeth this morning's lesson.' He took a deep breath and turned, and slowly walked back to his chair, not looking in the headmaster's direction, as he knew a disapproving look would be all he could expect.

Once back in the study the headmaster said, 'And what was that all about Appleyard?'

'I'm sorry sir, it's the first time in front of the whole school, and I was a bit nervous. I think that's why I tended to go a bit too fast.'

'Too fast! You would have won the three thirty at Haydock Park if you had been running.'

'I'll be OK for the rest of the week, now that I've got the first one out of the way. I'm sure I will.'

'We're taking no chances. See Mr Jackson sometime this morning, and he'll give you some tips and coaching.'

Mr Jackson was an English teacher who specialized in drama. After school that day they spent half an hour in the hall, and Ken was shown how to control his breathing and project his voice better. The rest of the week went without a hitch. When his turn came around again later in the year he found himself a little hesitant at first but he managed to get through without disgracing himself again.

Ken didn't expect the headmaster to remember this particular incident but, if anything, Ken had liked him even more than he did before for the kindly and humorous way he had handled it.

It was not an interview really. Just a chat about the school and things generally. The head had thought the school particularly strong during Ken's time there, when Ken had mentioned some of the teachers who had taught him. During his time at university Ken had attended an old-students' reunion dinner, at which a presentation was made to a master who was about to retire after thirty-five years at the school. In his speech of thanks he described how he came to teach at Barnfield Grammar School. As a young teacher in the south he had no real desire to move north, but a chance of promotion was on offer at Barnfield. Even so, he did not really wish to go there. As he left home on a cold snowy winter's morning to attend the interview he had told his wife that there was no chance of his accepting a post in a dismal coal-mining area, but that the interview experience would be valuable. She had looked relieved when he had said this. When he arrived home late that evening she could not believe the transformation and the news. He had accepted the job and was starting after Easter. Apparently the head of department and headmaster had so impressed and inspired him that he just could not refuse the offer. His wife took some persuading, but thirty-five years on she had no regrets apparently.

So this was how these people had been attracted to this school. National figures from the worlds of politics, arts, science and industry were always present to dispense their wisdom and give out the prizes at speech days. No doubt the head's influence was at work here as well. Ken's father always missed a shift at the pit to attend speech days with his mother.

Ken had already had one interview for a teaching post, but didn't know the result. His headmaster had been in touch with the education office and informed him that the head at the school he had been to first was keen to have him, and as the vacancy at his own school was only for one term he thought he could not really poach him. Ken duly heard from the education office and accepted the offer. His rows with his mother about leaving Tomlinsons abated when she realized he was not going to change his mind. His boss Jack Pearson, the chief chemist at the glassworks, had also tried to dissuade him. The results of the report had turned out much as Ken had anticipated once he had realized Jack's attitude. Certainly the lab had been vindicated to Jack's satisfaction, and some progress made, but Ken felt much more could have been made if one or two risks had been taken. Ken had decided not to kick against the pricks, and did not pursue it any further with Jack. His earlier confrontations had made him realize what a waste of time that would have been. It had come as a shock to him at the time, but on reflection he thought that he should have known this all along, because he knew Jack pretty well by now. To be fair, he also thought that Jack was probably right. After all, he knew the company and the personalities involved far better than Ken. When he left he didn't feel at all bitter about him, because Jack had always been helpful and considerate to him. In fact Ken apologized to him about the earlier troubles on the day he left.

On his last afternoon, Jack asked him into his office for a private chat.

'I'd just like to wish you well, Ken, in your new adventure, and thank you for the work you've done here. You'll be missed, you know.'

'It's kind of you to say so. I'll miss being here, but you've built a strong team around you. I would just like to say a couple of things if I may.'

'Sure, Ken.'

'First I'd like to say I'm sorry about getting a bit shirty with you about that report. I went over the top. I know that now. I thought you were very decent in the circumstances. Some chaps would have been a lot harder on me, and rightly so. I've got to learn not to be so hot-headed.'

'You're young, Ken. Think nothing of it.'

'Also, thanks for all your help whilst I've been here. You've a lot of patience, and I'd just like you to know I've noticed it and that it's been appreciated.'

'Thanks a lot, Ken. I'm very pleased we're parting on good terms. It would have been a pity if that report business had soured our friendship. I'll tell you this though, I think you've got guts to change direction like you are doing. I don't think I could ever have contemplated such a move.'

'I'm not sure if it's guts or that I'm just plain crazy. As the time to leave has approached I'm beginning to think the latter is the case.'

They both laughed.

25

THERE WERE only two other people in the doctor's waiting room when Ken entered. He had deliberately left it late to set off in order to try and avoid sitting there for an hour or two. He had arranged to have the statutory medical before going teaching, and the doctor suggested attending at the end of surgery one evening.

'Good evening doctor,' said Ken as he entered.

'Ah, Kenneth, hello, nice to see you. You'll be the last.'

'I am. Had a busy day?'

'I have indeed. Not much spare time once we get into December, especially with this damp foggy weather. Bronchitis is raging as usual. It'll be the medical, is it?'

'Yes, that's it. Shall I strip off?'

'Just to the waist. Then I'll want a urine sample, and all you will have to do then is pop to the hospital for a chest x-ray.'

As he was getting dressed again the doctor said, 'Your mother doesn't seem too happy about you changing jobs.'

'I didn't know she'd mentioned it to you doctor,' said Ken, a little surprised.

'Yes, when she was here last week.'

'What's wrong with the old hypochondriac now?'

'Kenneth, Kenneth, that's no way to speak about your mother.'

'Sorry, doctor, but she is a bit that way, you must admit.'

'No more than most. She only came for her three-monthly blood pressure check, and as it was up a little she mentioned your disagreements as a possible cause.'

'We've had one or two rows, but she's reconciled to it now. She worries unnecessarily.'

'She's only thinking of your welfare, remember that.'

'I know and I do, but it's difficult at times.'

As he was getting dressed again . . .

The doctor looked at the questionnaire which had to be completed.

'Now, Kenneth, just refresh my memory. What illnesses have you had? There doesn't seem to be much in the records.'

'Only the usual children's ones – measles, chicken pox etc. – and a bit of hay fever in the summer.'

'No operations of any kind?'

'No. Not unless you count that septic big toe.'

The doctor laughed at this.

'No. I only had to lance that, so we don't class that as an operation,' he said. Ken blushed slightly as he remembered the occasion.

'I was embarrassed about that, you know.'

'Why Kenneth?'

'Well, it seemed so trivial at the time. If you remember, I came to your house about eight o'clock one Sunday evening. You lanced it and gave me some antibiotic tablets. I felt a right idiot, pestering you at that time, but my dad would insist. At the time I didn't understand why, but I've since discovered the reason and have felt better about it. Let me tell you.'

'I didn't mind at all. But go on, I'd like to know why. I must admit that at the time I was a bit puzzled and thought it could have waited till Monday morning.'

'Well, I'd been on holiday and had arrived back home at Sunday tea-time. I just happened to mention that I'd had a septic big toe for a few days. Dad went spare when he saw it, and insisted I come to see you straight away. He wouldn't take no for an answer. I got to know later that he'd lost a brother who had a septic toe, from knocking it in the pit, which had gone the wrong way. Apparently it had all happened very quickly and he'd died within days. When he saw my toe he just panicked.'

'I see. We wouldn't have these sulpha drugs in those days,' he said, tapping a tin on his desk. "May and Baker"

208

was printed on the top of the label, and around the middle SULPHATRIAD in bold green lettering.

'Are those the ones known as M & Bs, the things that saved Churchill's life during the war?'

'The very ones. You must have missed your father a lot since he died. I know you were very close.'

'I have that, and more so at times like these when I need his advice and just somebody to talk to.'

'You see, Kenneth, there's something you probably haven't realized.'

'What's that?'

'Well, when he died you didn't just lose your father, but you lost your best friend as well – two in one so to speak.'

Ken pondered what the doctor had said.

Eventually he said, 'You know, I'd never looked at it like that before, but I think I know what you mean.'

'Being gregarious like you are has helped you a lot. I've kept in touch with how you've been from your mother. I happen to think that you're doing the right thing. Had you attempted it say twelve months ago, I would have had reservations. But I'm sure you'll be OK now. I've told your mother so.'

'That's good of you. She'll listen to you.'

'And you are courting, I hear?'

'I've met a very nice girl. Nothing serious – we just see each other now and again. But I really like her. I'm not rushing things though.'

'Quite right. But it's good for you at this stage in your life, and I was pleased to hear about it.'

'Thanks doctor. Look, I'm keeping you from your tea. I mustn't keep you any longer.'

'No, its OK. I always have it before I start evening surgery. I've enjoyed our little chat, for I haven't seen you for a long time. And all the best after Christmas in the new job. Health-wise you're fine. Remember the x-ray.'

'Many thanks doctor. Good-bye.'

Walking home he was thinking more about the two in one mentioned by the doctor. He had always liked Doctor Hughes. To Ken he had always seemed much more than a doctor. So friendly, so approachable – a doctor, family friend and philosopher all rolled into one. A disappearing breed if what you read in the newspapers was true.

'Well, what did Doctor Hughes say?' asked his mother when he returned home.

'Says I'm fit and well and have got to stop calling you a silly old hypochondriac.'

'Kenneth! What next?'

'I'm only kidding. Mind, you tell him some stuff, don't you? No, I'm OK he says, though he did say something interesting which I've been thinking about on the way home.'

'What was that?'

'He said that when dad died I also lost my best friend, as well as my father. I didn't like to ask him just what he meant. What do you think he meant?'

'Well, you were very close, and you are very much like him in your ways. Because of that I presume he meant it would be that much harder for you to get over his death.'

'We were close, but I didn't realize I was like him in my ways. Can you explain?'

'You're stubborn like he was. Once he was set on something, nothing could move him. Like at Millthorpe. I told him he'd upset a lot of people by standing for the union, but he wouldn't listen.'

'It strikes me that they wanted a shake-up from what I know about it. And anyway, it was instrumental in getting us to North Dene, so some good came out of it.'

'I've liked it here, I must admit. What do you think the doctor meant?'

'Well, more or less what you've said, but the doctor knew that he'd read widely and that I am probably missing talking to him about his intellectual interests. I didn't get

210

to know that side of him very well, because I was either too young or away at college. I am fascinated to know how he got into all that. I don't think you're much wiser than me on that one.'

'I'm not really. He always enjoyed reading, and then of course he met Andrew Murdoch. They had so much in common, and Andrew introduced him to ideas and writers he hadn't come across before. It was like putting a match to dry sawdust.'

Didn't Andrew get involved in the disputes at Millthorpe?'

'Well, he kept out of most of that. To go back to the business at Millthorpe, I think you ought to try and see both sides, you know. I liked living there as well, and had many friends. Although your father did mix with the other men at the club, he didn't join in things perhaps like he could have. As you know, he had a lovely tenor voice and did sing solo in the club. But he wouldn't join the choir. He did take a rather superior attitude at times, and this was resented by some. It was the same with the Union at the pit. Also, he did poke a bit too much fun at the pigeon-flyers. He did upset people, whereas I thought he should have compromised more. We did have a few battles about that. You're very much like him in that respect.'

'Funny is that. Do you remember when the poet C. Day Lewis came to speech day one year? His theme, if I remember rightly, was, 'Don't be scared to be a rebel. Be brave, have a go, be unpopular if necessary. I remember dad particularly enjoying him. No doubt he identified with it. I didn't see much of that side of him at North Dene.'

'No. He settled down and concentrated on his work, his reading and his horse-racing when we moved here. It affected him very deeply, what happened at Millthorpe. Andrew dying when he did made a big difference as well, of course.'

'I know he had very strong opinions about villages. He seemed to detest them. He never said much, but the odd times he did he couldn't disguise his feelings.'

'He did, that's true enough. He felt that no matter how long we lived at Millthorpe we would never be accepted fully because we hadn't been born there. He couldn't stand that kind of mentality at all. I agreed with him about that one. I think he would have lived in a tent before moving to live in another village. North Dene suited him fine.'

'I'm pleased you've put me in the picture more. It has been a puzzle to me since Percy mentioned that at the funeral. I'll also try to learn a few lessons from it, but you see if you don't tell me these things, how am I supposed to learn?'

'Well, I don't like raking up the past, but I think you've got a good point. It's just that I don't think you realize how much I miss him as well, and some of the memories are painful ones.'

'There were plenty of good ones though, as well.'

'Oh yes. Lots more of those than the others. So, as long as it's not too often, we'll have a chat about those from time to time. It'll be good for us both, I'm sure.'

'Agreed. I'm sure it will. I'll keep you to it.'

Ken had always been a little envious of his father's singing ability. He too had wished that he had been able to sing so well, but came face to face with reality in his first term at Barnfield Grammar School. In a music lesson one day the master gave each boy a voice test. They had to sing the first two verses of 'Early one morning, just as the sun was rising, I met a maiden singing in the valley below'. They were graded from A to D. Only Ken and one other boy were grade D voices. They were instructed, in future, to sit at the back of the class and if, during the singing, the class ever got low enough, to join in. They both ignored this advice and instead usually did their homework set for that evening during the music lesson. Ken had not seen his father sing in public very often, but he now found himself enjoying the thoughts of the occasion he found the most memorable. When Ken was twelve they had travelled north to Blaydon to attend the wedding of one of his cousins. For Ken the whole occasion was a real treat. He so rarely saw his grandparents and aunts and uncles and cousins. They made such a fuss of him. He loved every moment. But the wedding itself, particularly the reception and dancing afterwards, was truly magical. After the food, just about everybody seemed to perform a party piece. Some sang, some recited a short poem, others just a one-line rhyme appropriate for the occasion. The highlight for Ken, and for the others it seemed, was when his father stood and sang, looking at his cousin, his favourite song, 'Rose of England'. The emotion was almost tangible.

26

THE TRANSITION to teaching was not easy. Ken accepted the first school, and although he sensed that the head of the school and the heads of the Mathematics and Science departments in which he would be teaching had reservations, they were happy to have him. Such was the acute shortage of teachers in those subjects at that time. 'Meet us half-way,' seemed to be their attitude, 'and we can make things work out alright.' He got the impression that he would get plenty of help and understanding in the first few weeks, and this helped him to relax as the time drew close for him to start. He had many conversations with Ray about the problems likely to arise, although at that time Ray was having plenty of problems of his own at his school. A new head of department had arrived on the scene, and Ray resented the way in which he wanted to change everything. To Ken it sounded more like a straightforward personality clash than that, and thought Ray had not recognized the fact. Ray's personal life had its compensations though, for his relationship with Pat was going from strength to strength.

Ken was due to start after the Christmas holiday. He arranged to leave Tomlinsons two weeks before the school's end of term so that he could visit the school, collect the textbooks he would be using, meet some of the staff, and watch one or two lessons to let him get the feel of the place.

Watching the practised ease of the experienced teachers did make him feel a little apprehensive. The school was a recently-built mixed secondary modern, in a mining village six miles from Barnfield. It was administered by the West Riding of Yorkshire Education Authority. The facilities were excellent. The two main things that Ken noticed were the girls and the general ambience of the place. Girls had been absent from his secondary education, and he was wondering if it was this or other factors that made the school seem much lighter and more relaxed in atmosphere than his old school.

The butterflies in his stomach on the first morning were not helped when he walked into the headmaster's study. The head and deputy head, a woman considerably younger than the head, were poring over a time-table which covered the whole of the desk. When Ken entered they both looked up momentarily, said good morning, but then gave their attention back to the timetable. They were both looking very puzzled. After five minutes of this the penny dropped.

'This is last term's,' said the deputy, exasperated.

The head stared hard at the timetable with disbelief.

'My God, it is! I've picked up the wrong one.'

'Why? Where's this term's?' asked the deputy.

'At home. I'll just have to go and fetch it.'

He put on his overcoat and disappeared without another word being spoken. The deputy shook her head and smiled at Ken.

'It's typical is that, you know. He's just getting more and more forgetful. He won't be long though. He only lives fifteen minutes drive away. Come on. We'll go and tell the others.'

Ken followed her along the corridor to the staffroom.

The news was greeted with much mirth. It was decided to leave the children in the playground. As it was a bright dry day, this presented no problems. The staff were quite happy to continue relating to each other what they had done at Christmas.

Ken was sought out by the Head of Maths. He informed him that they had arranged for him to do no teaching that day, but just observe. The headmaster would see him after morning assembly to put him more in the picture. When

The Head stared hard at the timetable with disbelief.

he started to put him in the picture, Ken got a shock.

'You did say you could teach some Technical Drawing, didn't you?' said the head.

Ken had never said this, but did not like to say so. In fact he had never ever done this subject at school.

Before he could gather his thoughts and reply, the head continued, 'Only six periods a week I've put you down for, and only with the first two years.'

He passed Ken his timetable. The rest of his teaching week was equally divided between Maths and General Science, and there were a few blank spaces which were obviously free periods. He explained to him how he wished him to spend his first day. He seemed so kind and considerate that Ken just could not bring himself to mention about the Technical Drawing. He tried to approach the subject tangentially.

'When I came to see you before Christmas I didn't get any Technical Drawing textbooks.'

'Didn't you? Well, perhaps the best thing for you to do this morning before break is go and see Mr Hardacre about them. You'll find him in the Woodwork room.'

Mr Hardacre was sitting at his desk, marking books. The children were engaged at the benches. The room had a start of term look to it – the blackboard freshly cleaned, everything else spic and span and in its place.

'The Head's sent me for the Technical Drawing textbooks I'm to use this term. It seems he forgot to give them to me when I came last term.'

Mr Hardacre just raised his eyebrows and smiled. He hurriedly put out his pipe, saying as he did so, 'I know I shouldn't, but just now and then I can't resist. The head's very decent about it. Textbooks? Let me see?'

He went to a bookcase and returned with a slim book about half an inch thick.

'You could find this useful, but I work from these.'

He picked up a pile of papers from his desk.

'I've made my own exercise sheets. I've found that over the years the kids learn better from these and oral work than wading through textbooks.'

Ken took a quick glance at the first exercise. 'Nothing familiar there,' he thought, in a slight panic.

'Start them off with some Simple Orthographic Projection,' said Mr Hardacre.

The thought flashed through Ken's mind that perhaps they went to the local cinema for this lesson.

'What about the second years?' said Ken.

'They're into more theory, but still doing Orthographic Projection. The sheets all follow on in sequence. You'll quickly see where they've got to.'

Ken flicked through the sheets. He relaxed a little. The theory seemed to be geometry, which he was used to. He stayed in the Woodwork room until the break, spending the time chatting with Mr Hardacre but also going around the class, having a word with the children about their work. The rest of the day followed a similar pattern, but the Maths and Science he felt at home with. He was given one other slim book that day – a laboratory manual from one of the Science teachers.

'People like me and you would much rather settle down in the evenings with a book like this than a novel,' he said as he passed it to him. This time Ken's eyebrows raised, though he did not let the teacher notice. Ken had never heard most of the world's literature dismissed in quite this way before. Ken thanked him for his trouble, and the manual certainly came in useful in the weeks to follow.

That evening Ken attempted to discover what Simple Orthographic Projection was. At first it did not look very simple, but with the aid of Mr Hardacre's sheets he felt confident he could make a start. Luck was on his side, because he had no Technical Drawing lessons the following day.

The first few weeks were very hard work. He spent most

218

evenings preparing lessons for the following day. The headmaster's advice, when he first discussed becoming a teacher, he found invaluable.

'Preparation, that's the secret, even if it's only five minutes. It will make all the difference.'

Ken certainly found this to be the case, for on the odd occasion when he could not find the time for this the lesson never seemed to go as well. On the whole the other teachers were friendly towards him, although one or two did seem to resent the fact that he had no proper teaching qualifications. He was not the only teacher on the staff so qualified, but as the others had been teaching for many years this seemed to have been forgotten in their case. Had he not been there the rest of them would, apparently, have had fewer free periods in which to mark and prepare. The majority were pleased for that reason alone. Easter seemed to arrive very quickly that year. Ken felt ready for a break, but also rather pleased with himself. He was finding his feet and feeling much more relaxed by then.

Discipline problems were only encountered with some of the fourth and fifth year boys. They were trying it on because he was new. Ken had done plenty of this himself, so he did not think too badly about them. He gave much thought to deciding how to solve it, and he asked for guidance from his colleagues. They had all, it seemed, worked out methods to suit themselves. But he found many of their tips helpful. It persisted though until one of the P.T. and Games masters was absent through illness. Ken had known the senior Games master, through cricket, before he started teaching there. He asked Ken if he would mind giving up one or two of his free periods to help out. Ken jumped at the chance, just to have a break. As he was walking up to the playing fields to take a double period of football, two of the troublemakers started to bait him.

'I don't suppose you know the rules, Sir, do you? You

219

teach us Maths. I bet you know nowt about football,' said one.

'It'll be a reight waste of time with him teking us,' he heard another say.

Ken had already changed into his track suit in the school, but was carrying his boots in a small holdall. He intended changing into these in the groundsman's hut near the field.

'Got yer sandwiches in there, Sir?' the first one said.

Ken remained silent, but these taunts gave him an idea. He had intended, at first, to act only as referee, but now he decided to join in the action occasionally; selected interventions when the opportunity arose. In the hut he took off his track suit bottom and put on his boots. The boys all looked surprised. The boots were well worn, well cleaned and dubbined, but they were also one of the most popular makes of boot on the market at that time. He now actually looked like a footballer. In the preliminary warm-up before having a game, Ken only touched the ball twice. It came to him, on each occasion, when he was standing on the edge of the penalty area. The first time he hit it hard and true (with his right foot) straight at the boy in the goal, who tipped it over the bar and then wrung his hands at the pain. The second time he rattled a shot against a post with his left foot. The boys again looked surprised.

'Tha' can be on our side,' the cheeky one said.

'Speak properly, lad,' Ken retorted.

'Sorry, sir.'

In the game that followed, Ken first helped one side and then the other to try and make an entertaining even match of it. He chose when and who to tackle very carefully. The bother-causers left the field covered in mud, bruised and chastened. After that he had a much better rapport with them and his Maths lessons were more orderly. There is more than one way of skinning a cat, he mused to himself as they made their way back to the school.

The Technical Drawing lessons did present problems, but he solved these by keeping three sheets in front of the boys. Mr Hardacre was quite happy with the progress made, and the summer examination results were well up to standard. He soon found that he was enjoying the Science and Maths. Even when he overheard a first year boy remark to his friend, as they passed his desk at the end of a Maths lesson, that he was not going to worry about his results too much – he could always become a dustman! Ken particularly liked this boy because, although he struggled with Maths, he did try very hard and was always polite and handed in his work on time.

27

ONE MONDAY AFTERNOON, just before Easter, Tony called at Ken's house but found that he had not arrived home from school.

'He's not home yet, Tony, but come in anyway, he won't be long,' said Mrs Appleyard.

'Thanks, I will if you don't mind, Mrs Appleyard.'

'Would you like a cup of tea?'

'It would be very welcome, and you know me, I never refuse a drink.'

'Yes, but it's usually stronger stuff than this,' she said, laughing.

Tony laughed with her.

'Aren't you working today?' she asked, as she poured the tea.

'I have been, but I usually start at six in the mornings, so I get home about three o'clock. Most of our contracts are with the Coal Board, and we find that it fits in with them if we make an early start.'

'How's your mother and father? I don't seem to have seen them for a while. Is her arthritis still playing her up?'

'They're OK thanks. She has good and bad days with that. It seems to depend on the weather. She's not the complaining type though; she just takes it in her stride.'

'She's always been like that has your mum, as long as I've known her, and that's a long time now.'

'Ken's taken to teaching OK so far, hasn't he?'

'He has, I'm pleased to say. I did have doubts about him leaving Tomlinsons, but he does seem more content, I've got to admit. He really likes it. I never thought he would have the patience for a job like that.'

'He never was a stick-in-the-mud, Ken, you know. He always loved a challenge when he was a lad, and he doesn't seem any different now. I don't think I could ever contemplate such a big change of direction. Alright, I'll probably move around a bit, but it would have to be civil engineering and something I'm experienced in.'

'You know, we're all so proud of how the children in this small estate have turned out. Whoever would have thought that so many of you would have got to university? It was unheard of in our day for working-class children, as all you are, to do that.'

'We've been lucky, that's what, Mrs Appleyard.'

'Lucky? How do you mean? You've all worked very hard if you ask me. How do you mean, lucky?'

'In our choice of parents and schools, that's what I mean. We were encouraged and allowed to stay on at school. And look at the schools we went to; you'll not find any much better. I know the grammar school has its critics, but if you could cope with the academic work it was marvellous. Perhaps it wasn't so good for the ones who struggled academically, but even so the ones I know in that category are all doing well. I'm sure they all got a good education.'

'They were good, that's true. We certainly were happy with them.'

'To change the subject, and I don't want to pry, but how's Ken's love life? He's very cagey about it and doesn't tell us much.'

'I've met her you know, the girl from Burnside, and I like her. I think it has helped Kenneth settle down to teaching, and keeps him out of the pubs as well. I don't think it's too serious just yet, but they have been seeing more of each other lately.'

Tony looked a bit sheepish at the reference to the pubs, but then continued, 'I've come, really, to see if Ken will come to the pub tonight, to help us pick the football teams for the weekend.'

'But he's not on the selection committee, Tony.'

'No. Well, we want to co-opt him if he's prepared, because Ray can't make it tonight and it does look as though he could miss a few weeks.'

'Whyever not?' she asked, looking alarmed.

'I don't really know. I've got the story second-hand, and not much of it either. His brother called at home and told my mother that he had been taken ill, and asked her to let me know that he couldn't come tonight and probably wouldn't be able to play for a few weeks. Mum did ask for more details, but Peter wouldn't say anything. I thought of going to their house, but in the circumstances thought that I'd better not.'

'I haven't heard anything. He was here only last Thursday evening. He must have been here all of two hours, mainly talking about work. He's been wonderful to Kenneth, you know. He's a lovely lad is Ray. He was fine then; whatever can have happened to him? I know he drives too fast and drinks too much. I wonder if he's had an accident?'

'No, it's not that; Mum asked Peter if it was that.'

'Perhaps Kenneth will have heard something at school today. I do hope it's nothing serious. Something always seemed to be happening to him when he was a boy.'

'I'll have to be off, Mrs Appleyard. Mum will have the tea ready. If Ken can make it, the meeting starts at eight o'clock. Thanks for the tea.'

Tony got up and made his way to the back door.

'I know he's not going out tonight, so I'm sure he'll come, Tony, especially when he hears about Ray. Cheerio then. Remember me to your mother and father.'

'I will. Cheerio.'

* * *

Having tea, Ken's mother told him Tony's news. He had not heard anything at school, and was as puzzled as they were.

'The last time I saw him was at the dance on Saturday night. He was with Pat as usual, and he was OK then, though Pat did seem very subdued, I thought. She's usually bright and bubbly, but when we were with them she was much quieter than normal, though Ray was much the same as ever.'

'He's been going out with her a long time now.'

'Six months, actually. It's a long time, is that, for Ray.'

'What's she like?'

'Very, very nice.'

'Do you mean in looks, or as a person?'

'Well, both. I don't know her that well, but she's certainly nice looking, and does seem a genuinely nice person. I may be wrong, of course.'

'It's always Ray who's in the wars, isn't it? As a lad his mother was forever taking him to the casualty department to be stitched up and have plasters put on his broken limbs. It always seems to be the nice ones who come a cropper,' his mother said, very dejectedly.

'Look, it may not be too serious. Let's not jump to any conclusions until we know the facts. He's probably just got a bad attack of shingles, or something equally innocuous.'

'I think Peter would have told Tony's mother if that had been the case. It's funny why he wouldn't say much about it.'

'It is. Look, when I've finished my tea I'm going up to their house to see what it's all about. Then I'll go to the meeting from there.'

'Do you think you should? Tony thought of that but decided against it. I got the impression he thought it might be embarrassing.'

'Tony's never gone to Ray's very much. I've always gone there since being a kid; it won't be embarrassing for me. Mrs Evans is more likely to be annoyed with me for not going. It's been like a second home for me as long as I can remember.'

225

'It has, but be tactful, mind.'

'I will. Going back to what you asked about Pat has reminded me about something. You know, Tony doesn't care for her at all.'

'Why?'

'He thinks she's a bit stuck up and snobbish.'

'Has he told Ray this?'

'Yes. Tony's not shy at saying what he thinks.'

'And how did Ray react?'

'Just laughed and told him to stick to barmaids.'

'What do you think about that?'

'Well, I could see what Tony was driving at, but she's always been alright with me. Tony can be a bit crude at times you know; she probably doesn't care for him – and it shows. Even allowing for that, though, I think he's got a point.'

'Have you talked to Ray about it? He'd listen to you more than Tony.'

'Yes I have, but Ray couldn't or wouldn't accept it at all.'

'Love is blind, as they say.'

'Could be. He is rather besotted with her.'

'So bad, is it?'

'Oh yes. I've never ever known him like he's been these last few months. Literally on cloud nine.'

'But he's been having problems at work.'

'Yes, but those haven't bothered him very much. Normally I think they would have, but he's coped with them very easily in his present state of mind.'

'Let's hope then that it's got nothing to do with Pat.'

'I'll agree with that.'

Getting washed and then sitting reading the paper after tea, Ken felt sure that this business could only be connected with Pat. From the first he had felt Pat did not have the feelings for Ray that Ray had for her. Ray's mother had also voiced the same opinion to Ken, but Ken had not liked to say so. He had hoped to be proved wrong. He could not concentrate on the paper, but found himself mulling over recent events to see if any clues were there to suggest what might have happened. Pat had been quiet on Saturday night, but that was the only thing he could come up with. Now he was thinking how pleased he had been to have known Ray and the Evans family for most of his life. They had come from North Wales when Mr Evans found work in the mines of South Yorkshire. It was true that, as a boy, Ray had been accident prone, but not a lot more than the rest of them. He had more accidents because he had more ideas to try out and put into practice than the others, thought Ken. Surely the same pattern was not going to follow him into manhood.

28

WALKING UP THE STREET to Ray's, Ken realized that this was the only time he had not looked forward to going there. Now he was having second thoughts. Would he be interfering in things that did not concern him? On balance he felt compelled to go, if only for a couple of minutes. He knocked on the back door, and it was answered by Mrs Evans. She looked upset, but her face brightened at the sight of Ken.

'Hello, Kenneth, you've heard then? Come in.'

'Well, I only know that Ray's not well. Tony called to ask me if I would go to the meeting tonight to take Ray's place as he was ill. I'm on my way there now and thought I'd pop in just to see what the problem is. I hope you don't mind?'

'Not at all. I'm pleased to see you.'

Ray's younger brother and sister were in the living room, and Mrs Evans told them to go into the front room so that she could talk to Ken.

When they had left the room, she said, 'They're too young to understand, but even so they are very upset. They've never seen Ray like this before.'

'Like what, Mrs Evans? I'm in the dark you know.'

'Well I'm in the dark as well, Ken, really.'

She proceeded to tell him what had happened. Pat had told Ray, late on Saturday night, that she did not want to see him any more. Ray had been agitated on Sunday morning when he had told his mother this, but at that time had not taken Pat too seriously, thinking that she was just a bit fed up and would change her mind. Thinking this he had gone to see her on Sunday afternoon. Doctor Allsop from Bradstone was there. Apparently Pat had been having an affair with him for the last two months.

'But he's married with two children,' interrupted Ken at this point.

'I think it's that that has upset Ray the most. As you know, he worshipped the ground she walked on and the thought of losing her would have been bad enough, but this on top I think has been just too much for him.'

'Why? What happened on Sunday afternoon?'

'There was a big scene and a lot of shouting, and from what I can gather Ray called them both some lovely names. He was heartbroken when he came home for his tea. He couldn't stop crying.'

'Where is he now? Has he been to school today?'

'In bed; he won't get up. No, he isn't fit to go to work. I asked the doctor to call this morning.'

'What did he say?'

'All he told me was that he was suffering from a kind of shock and anxiety. He spoke to Ray on his own for most of the time. Ray won't tell me what he said – perhaps he'll tell you, Ken. He did leave a prescription for some tablets which he said would help to calm him down. He hardly slept at all last night.'

'Do you think I could have a quick word with him?'

'I'd like you to, but don't know if he will. I'll go and ask him.'

After a few minutes she returned.

'At first he said no, but I've persuaded him. I'll go in the other room, I think that will be best.'

Ken was taken aback, but he tried to conceal this when Ray came down. Normally, Ray was dapper and immaculate, but standing at the door to the living room, unshaved, his black curly hair dishevelled and his eyes bulging, he looked rather pathetic. Seeing Ken he looked at his feet and hesitated.

'Hello, Ray – not so good old lad? Come on, sit down and tell me about it if you want. If you don't, that's OK. I'll understand.'

229

They sat in armchairs on either side of the coal fire.

'Mam's told you what went off at the weekend?'

'Yes. I'm sorry Ray, I really am.'

Ray did not reply, but tears welled up in his eyes. They both sat staring at the fire. Eventually Ken broke the silence.

'The doctor came to see you this morning. What did he say?'

'Not much. Told me to start worrying after the sixth time this happens, not the first. I'm not made that way, Ken. You know that.'

'I know. He'd only be doing his best to help, Ray, I'm sure.'

'I expect so, but I just can't see it like that.'

Ken stayed chatting to him for another thirty minutes, but it was difficult because every few minutes or so Ray got to his feet and walked around the room rubbing his hair, very agitated, and lighting a cigarette which he only half smoked before throwing it on the fire.

'Look, I'll call in again tomorrow night — I'm going to the pub now to help pick the teams,' said Ken as he left.

Ray saw him to the door, and then started to go back upstairs.

'Thanks for coming, Ken. See you tomorrow.'

They sat in armchairs on either side of the coal fire.

29

As HE MADE HIS WAY to the North Dene Arms, Ken felt at a loss. He had never seen Ray, or anyone else for that matter, in such a state. The landlord let them use a small side-room for their meetings, and Ken got himself a pint of bitter and had a deep drink before joining the others.

'Pleased you could make it,' said Tony.

'Sorry I'm a bit late. I called to see Ray.'

Ken briefly related what he knew. As he finished, Tony said, scornfully, 'Is that all it is? I always said she wasn't worth it.'

Ken exploded.

'Is that all you can say? I've never heard anything as selfish in all my life. Mind, I shouldn't have expected anything else from you.'

By now, Ken was visibly shaking with rage. The others glanced towards Tony to see how he would react. He took a drink of his beer. This outburst had surprised him. Ken also had a drink, and he tried to compose himself. Tony's remark had touched a raw nerve.

'I don't know what I said to deserve that,' said Tony, eventually.

'If you'd seen him you'd perhaps understand better.'

'Why?' asked Tony.

'He's in a right mess. He can't stop shaking, he can't sit still, and he's chain-smoking.'

'Oh. I didn't realize he was so bad,' said Tony. They selected the teams and then Tony and Ken walked home together.

'Look, Tony, I'm sorry if I went overboard earlier. Seeing Ray like that was a shock. I'm sorry if I offended you.'

'Forget it. I think I understand how you must have felt

232

at the time. You and Ray have always been very close. You've got to admit that I've been proved right about her.'

'I know you didn't like her, but I don't think you could have predicted something like this would happen.'

'I'm not too sure. She seemed two-faced to me, and with people like that you can expect anything.'

'I suppose so. Anyway, what are we going to do about it?'

'What can we do? There's no way she'll change her mind.'

'I know that. I mean what are we going to do about Ray?'

'Surely that's for the doctor and his family to sort out.'

Listening to this last remark, Ken now felt pleased with himself for having had a go at Tony earlier. He did not pursue the matter any further with him, but changed the subject to the forthcoming weekend's games.

30

OVER THE NEXT weeks and months, Ray seemed to make very little progress. Going to work became very hard indeed. There were times when he could not go at all. His family, the doctors, and his friends, barely knew how to help, such was his distress. His sporting activities ground to a halt. In order to see him, Ken and the others visited him at home. Realizing his plight, Tony also spent many hours with him. To them he looked to be going round and round in circles, so obsessed was he by what had happened. They thought they might be helping by just being there and listening to him, but did not feel confident that this was the case because it was hard to see any improvement. It was as though a volcano had erupted inside him, so suddenly that it had wrought a permanent change in his personality. The carefree, laughing, full of life boy and young man had been changed into an anxious, depressed, confused individual who could hardly cope with life at all. Six months it was before he started to improve, but even then it was a slow, painful, process. They managed to get him playing soccer again and going for the occasional drink.

At about this time Ken bumped into Pat in Barnfield one evening. She had looked away as though to try and avoid him. But he spoke to her as she approached.

'Hello there. How's things? Not seen you for a long time.'

She stopped and coloured slightly.

'Hello Ken, how are you?'

'Fine thanks.'

They were standing about fifty yards from the entrance to the Imperial Hotel, and after a few perfunctory remarks Ken suggested buying her a drink. She readily agreed. He bought a gin and tonic and a glass of bitter, and they resorted to a quiet corner of the lounge.

'Are you still teaching?' she asked.

'Yes, and enjoying it now. I think I've got the worst over. What about you – still with the drug company?'

'Same job, different company. I had a better offer from one of their rivals and accepted it. Are you still courting?'

'Yes and no. One week it's on, then it's off – one of those kinds of relationships. My mother likes her and thinks I should settle down, but I'm not too sure. I'm in no hurry to get married.'

There was a lull in the conversation which Ken broke, saying, 'No doubt you heard about Ray?'

'Well I did hear he hadn't been well. How is he now?'

'Improving slowly. He's gone through a grim time. I don't think he can understand it himself, and I and the rest of his friends certainly can't make much sense of it, though we have tried, for his sake.'

'What did the doctors say?'

'To begin with they just thought it would be a two-day wonder kind of thing, but when it lasted so long and they saw how ill and distressed he was they told his parents that he was suffering something similar to a bereavement. I don't understand these things very much, but I could see their point.'

'Do you blame me, Ken?'

Ken studied, and then sipped his beer before answering.

'No, not really.'

'The *not really* bit sounds as though you're not too sure.'

'It's a free country and you weren't engaged or anything, but ... '

She interrupted him before he could finish the sentence.

'But you think I should have told him sooner.'

235

'Yes.'

'I should have, I know. I tried, believe me I tried, but I had a sixth sense that something awful might happen when I did – mind I'd no idea it would be as bad as it was. The only thing I reproach myself for is not telling him as soon as I started seeing Doctor Allsop. Do you think that that had much to do with how Ray reacted?'

'I'm certain it did have some effect, but just how much I wouldn't like to say. He would have reacted badly in any event, but how much worse that made it I just don't know. Are you still seeing Doctor Allsop?'

'Occasionally. It's awful, Ken. Try to understand that. I'm in love with him and he's in love with me. Please try to see it from that point of view. I'm in a terrible predicament. Alright, I haven't fallen ill like Ray, but I've had sleepless nights and anguish, believe me. I've been very lonely in Barnfield. I've missed my friends at home – just someone to talk to and confide in – do you see?

'I do.'

During the whole of their conversation Ken found himself realizing more and more that he did not understand women very much. Until this time he thought that he understood them pretty well, but now he was having to re-assess. First his mother, then his own relationships, and now Pat. In some way girls had been excluded much of the time when he and his friends were boys, and perhaps they were paying the price for that now.

'I'd never met anybody quite like you three, you know,' said Pat.

'Which three?'

'You, Ray and Tony.'

'How do you mean?'

She laughed.

'Well, let me tell you what I used to call you when I wrote home.'

'What?'

236

'The Three Musketeers.'

They both laughed.

'You mean we haven't grown up yet and are showing no signs of doing so. A fair comment, I think.'

Ken had always realized the truth of the saying, 'Boys will be Boys', but until now it had never crossed his mind that 'Girls will be Girls'.

Also from Bridge Publications:

Echoing Hills

by Phyllis Crossland

A story of three generations of country folk living in the upper Don valley during the eighteenth and early nineteenth centuries.

Life on the homestead is hard; illness and death never far away; but Thomas and Ellen Brammer are strong enough to survive into old age. They end their days at Truns just as the gipsy predicted. Other prophecies relating to the families are also fulfilled, good and bad, through the next generations.

In an age of violence and brutality, the rural scene is not always peaceful. The Land Enclosure Act makes life difficult for Thomas's family, who turn to butchering as a means of augmenting their income. Their cottage neighbours are in worse straits. When a child is caught in a man-trap, murder ensues.

Railway builders, wire drawers and quarry workers influence the lives of the third generation at Truns. Friction and jealousy within the family lead to more unlawful killings.

The homestead at Truns passes out of the family when, much against his will, James is forced to leave by circumstances he cannot control. Yet, as the gipsy foretold to Ellen, their descendants do return to the place more than a century later. Thomas's footsteps are then retraced and the hills echo again with voices from the past.

*   *   *

Echoing Hills (ISBN 0 947934 20 0); hbk £12.95

From any bookseller or, in case of difficulty, by post (add £1.00) from the publishers.

While Martha Told the Hours
A South Yorkshire Tapestry

by Sheila Margaret Ottley

From the vantage point of her father's printing office with its many and varied customers, the author, as a child and teenager in the 'twenties and 'thirties, could observe and with her remarkable memory commit to mind the broad spectrum of happenings in Hoyland half a century ago.

This surprisingly detailed book, which touches also on earlier and later events and national issues relevant to life in Hoyland at that time, will fascinate not only those who possess first-hand knowledge of this corner of South Yorkshire but readers everywhere, who will find in it a microcosm of English life between the Wars.

*   *   *

'Rarely can any town ... have been so thoroughly documented.'
The Sheffield Star

'... an historical collection of facts and personal memories perfect for the local historian, schools or anybody who wants to find out about their home town: in fact no Hoyland household should be without one.'
South Yorkshire Times

'... an account of Hoyland life over the past 60 years, seen through her own eyes.'
Barnsley Chronicle

While Martha Told the Hours (ISBN 0 947934 17 0) pbk £10.95
(ISBN 0 947934 18 9) hbk £15.95

From any bookseller or, in case of difficulty, by post (add 60p or £1.00 respectively) from the publishers.

Also from Bridge Publications:

Between the Lines

by Alan W. Wootton

'You could say that it is the biography of a Derbyshire Railwayman. Or the story of a Belper farming family's daughter.

'In fact, it is the autobiography of their son – but it ends when he's not yet out of his schooldays.

'*Between the Lines* is a beautifully written fascinating story by Alan W. Wootton, retired surveyor, engineer and man of many parts. ... This delightful story is about the colourful life of his parents, particularly his railwayman father, known to all as Woody.

'Woody was born at Sawmills, near Ambergate, and was a regular soldier before and during the First World war in which his arm was so badly shattered that all medical advice was amputation.

'So he went round the battlefield hospitals until he found one, an American Army hospital, that said they would try to save it. That took more than a year, by which time the war was over.

'Mr Wootton writes his story like a train journey, with chapter headings such as Dep. Derbyshire, Wayside Halt, and Branch Lines.

* * *

'Written in a highly readable and pleasingly different style, the book successfully conveys a convincing impression of working class life in England between the First and Second World Wars.'

South Yorkshire Times

Between the Lines (ISBN 0 947934 27 8) pbk £7.50,
(ISBN 0 947934 28 6) hbk £12.95

From any bookseller or, in case of difficulty, by post (add 60p pbk or £1.00 hbk) from the publishers.

Also from Bridge Publications:

Cricket-Stumps and Sticklebacks
A Childhood on Teesside

by Don Smith

This is more than just a tale of youthful frolics in that area of north-
east England which is usually associated with the River Tees. As well
as capturing in words the landscape and environmental characteristics
of the part of the country described, it also conveys an impression of
the unique personality of the local population. These aspects of Teesside will be recognized both by readers of this book who know the area
as it is today and by those who remember it as it was in the 'twenties
and 'thirties, when the incidents and events described took place.

Childhood memories belong to us all. Happy and sad occasions easily
slip away into oblivion. This fascinating tale will remind you of times
long forgotten. Half-remembered pleasures, places and faces will be
recalled.

Births, birthdays, deaths, Christmas, holidays, visiting relatives. These
are all events which have a long-   lasting influence upon young
lives. This story includes many such items.

*   *   *

Cricket-Stumps and Sticklebacks (ISBN 0 947934 23 5) pbk £9.95

From any bookseller or, in case of difficulty, by post (add 60p) from the
publishers.

Also from Bridge Publications:

Farmstead of the Britons
The Story of a West Riding Village

by John F. Wilkinson

This book tells the story of the village of West Bretton, of which Mr Wilkinson is a resident.

Midway between Barnsley and Wakefield and within five minutes' drive of Junction 38 of the M1 motorway, West Bretton is the home of the famous Yorkshire Sculpture Park (which houses a Henry Moore collection) and the Bretton Hall College of Higher Education.

In this book, the author traces the development of the village from Roman times to the horror of William the Conqueror's 'Wasting of the North' and the devastating effect this policy had in the area.

The book looks at the slow revival from this policy and further changes caused by such momentous events as the Black Death, the Wars of the Roses, the Civil War and the Industrial Revolution.

It also looks at the overwhelming social changes of the past seventy years caused by the form of taxation necessary to fund two terrible World Wars.

*   *   *

'This fascinating book . . . '
Barnsley Chronicle

'Mr Wilkinson has long been fascinated by his "roots".'
The Wakefield Express

Farmstead of the Britons (ISBN 0 947934 25 10) pbk £10.95
(ISBN 0 947934 18 9) hbk £9.95

From any bookseller or, in case of difficulty, by post (add 60p) from the publishers.

Also from Bridge Publications:

Thinking It Out
Christianity in Thin Slices

by Ian Dunlop

For almost twenty years the author, a Canon and the Chancellor of Salisbury Cathedral, answered readers' queries in the *Church Times*. This book comprises a selection of his answers on subjects as wide-ranging as 'How to Start Praying', 'Faith and Reason', 'Hymns with Everything?', 'True Penitence' and 'The Authority of the Bible'.

A reader once asked him to condemn outright the modern attitude to sex. Canon Dunlop replied: 'I do not write a column called *Laying Down the Law*. My column is entitled *Thinking It Out*.' In these short articles he is often happy to leave a question virtually unsolved, instead endeavouring to put the reader in a position to answer it himself. To elicit this kind of personal response is an integral part of his counselling technique. He also shows a rare ability to guide the enquirer direct to the heart of a philosophical problem, using simple, straightforward language and avoiding confusing the issue with religious jargon.

Newcomers to the faith and committed Christians, enquiring laymen and practising clergy, students searching for answers and teachers attempting to help them, will derive benefit and stimulus from the book each at his own level.

The author shows himself to be a sincere churchman, tolerant of most tenable shades of Christian belief, who maintains a balance between Church tradition and scripture, and the spiritual and secular facets of his faith, and is never at a loss to find an apt quotation in the great works of English literature.

*   *   *

'Thin slices, but containing much nourishment for mind and spirit.'
Church News

Thinking It Out (ISBN 0 947934 07 3) hbk £3.50
(ISBN 0 947934 06 5) pbk £6.50

From any bookseller or, in case of difficulty, by post (add 50p) from the publishers.

Also from Bridge Publications:

The Christmas Tree
A New Look at the Nativity Story

by Ethel Wallace

A delightfully-unusual version of the Nativity Story which deserves a place on every Christmas reading list.

The Christmas Tree, whilst being essentially a traditional account of the birth and childhood of Jesus, is told with a remarkable freshness and vitality appropriate to the late Twentieth Century. Even more remarkable is the fact that this is the work of a lady in her ninety-eighth year!

Ethel Wallace spent all her working life as a teacher, first at various schools in England, ending with eight years as Science and R.E. Mistress at Guildford High School; then for over twenty- five years in a Mission School in South Africa. She is a member of Oxford University and holds the Archbishop's licence to teach Theology. She has written this book for children and younger teenagers who have the capacity to think, in the hope that it may illuminate for them the doctrine of the incarnation. *The Christmas Tree* represents the historical fact, the tinsel and the baubles are the added trimmings, and the candles are the suggestions which throw light on some of the problems.

*   *   *

'She knows how to hold a young audience and teach without preaching . . . Her small booklet appears deceptively slight for the spirit of hope it contains.'
Church Times

The Christmas Tree (ISBN 0 947934 05 7) pbk £1.50

From any bookseller or, in case of difficulty, by post (add 50p) from the publishers.

Also from Bridge Publications:

The Penistone Scene

by R.N. Brownhill and J. Smethurst

The Penistone Scene has been compiled by Dick Brownhill with
assistance from local historian John Smethurst. Mr Brownhill has spent
much of his leisure time in recent years taking photographs and col-
lecting information about his home town of Penistone. His ancestor Mr
George Brownhill came to the Penistone area from Sheffield in 1749.
It was Dick's interest in his own past and that of his native town which
motivated him to compile the photographic collection which make up
The Penistone Scene. Penistone is a small market town, situated more
than 700 feet above sea level on the edge of the Pennines, and has a
history which can be traced back to Alfred the Great. However it is
probably the last 150 years which have seen the greatest changes in
the town, and it is this period which is reflected in 'The Penistone
Scene'. Penistone has a large number of historical buildings, markets,
an annual agricultural show and a whole host of other festivals and
events, many of which have been captured in photographs over the
years. *The Penistone Scene* brings to life the social history of this small
market town in a way which makes it of great interest now and, as our
small market towns are ever swallowed into cities, an important record
for the future.

*   *   *

The Penistone Scene (ISBN 0 947934 15 4) pbk £5.95

From any bookseller or, in case of difficulty, by post (add 75p) from the
publishers.

Also from Bridge Publications:

A House Divided
The Life and Death of John Billam of Thorpe Hesley

by Stephen Cooper

This is more than just a gripping tale of madness, avarice and family feuding. The author presents us with a cameo of life in an eighteenth century South Yorkshire village whose characters (blacksmith, cordwainer, maltster, farmer, gardener, labourer and domestic servant) each have a part to play in Billam's life and comment with homely wisdom on his story like the rustics in Thomas Hardy's Wessex novels.

In addition, *A House Divided* helps to place textbook history in perspective. During the years when these events occurred, Britain lost her American colonies, the French Revolution took place, and Napoleon beat his ignominious retreat from Moscow. Yet, just as today some minor crisis nearer home looms larger than cataclysmic events abroad, so two hundred years since in this corner of England, Billam commanded more attention than Bonaparte.

All the facts recorded in this book are true, unearthed in the course of meticulous research.

They serve, moreover, to prove the old adage that truth is frequently stranger than fiction.

They also have literary overtones. Deranged, and callously treated by his wife and daughters, John Billam, at the centre of events, is a village King Lear. Furthermore, the misfortunes which dog his self-seeking heirs after his death seem to possess the inevitability of nemesis in Greek tragedy.

*   *   *

*'... an important milestone in local history writing
in the South Yorkshire area ...*
The Hallamshire Historian

A House Divided (ISBN 0 947934 11 1) pbk £4.50
(ISBN 0 947934 12 X) hbk £8.95

From any bookseller or, in case of difficulty, by post (add 60p) from the publishers.